BACK
TO THE
RIDDERLANDS

BACK
TO THE
RIDDERLANDS

MELISSA RUTH ROTERT

To my big sister Sara and the relationship that wasn't always an easy one

Praise for Back To The Ridderlands

"*Back To The Ridderlands* continues the fun and fantasy of the Ridderlands series with a story told from Jess's perspective. With her sister's impending leave for college looming, Jess has some unresolved feelings to work out with Sue B about the fact that she's about to be left behind. And when Jess uses magic to meddle in Sue's relationship with Barnaby—and transport them all back to the Ridderlands—things get extra messy and complicated. Jess is smart and brave, and throughout their magical mishaps, she eventually comes to realize that she doesn't need Sue B to solve all her problems for her anymore. She's strong enough to stand on her own two feet."—Kelly Mangan, author of *Maeve Mulvaney Has Had Enough* (Holiday House). *Like That Eleanor* (Cardinal Rule Press)

"The perfect wrap-up for an endearing and engaging trilogy. A wonderful middle-grade story about trust, confidence, and growing into your own power. A magical ride back into a world of wonder. Readers are in for a treat!"—Dana Goldstein, author of the Dax Masters series books *Shift* and *Flow*

"A thrilling tale of sisterhood and self-discovery, *Back to the Ridderlands* is sure to captivate and inspire young readers. Filled with magic, danger, and heart, Jessie's perilous journey back into the Riddlerlands will keep the pages turning and the imagination burning."—Jaime Formato, author of *Roll For Initiative* (@RP_Kids)

Chapter One

There are some things that happen in a kid's life that they never forget, no matter how young they were when it happened. I was practically an infant the first time I rescued my sister and Barnaby from a flock of hungry ridders, giant pteranodons from another world. Only a year later, we were back in the same horrible place rescuing Barnaby's bestie who ended up being Mr. Ritter, a villainous janitor trying to trap us there. We'd probably all still be stuck in the Ridderlands—or worse, eaten—if it wasn't for my (now lost) magic powers and bravery.

But that was a super long time ago, back when my sister, Sue B, still called me Jessie Jess like the baby I was. Now, I basically rule Plank Street Elementary School and can't wait to move up to the fifth grade in three short months.

The problem is, at the end of the summer, I have to say goodbye to Sue B. Even though we're almost eight years apart, we actually get along super well. She lets me tag along when she goes shopping with her friends, drives me to get ice cream for dinner when Mom and Dad are both working, and doesn't make me feel like I'm annoying for wanting to be around.

Sue B goes to college next year. And she's not just going to one of the schools an hour away, where I might still get to spend time with her on weekends. She's going all the way to the other side of the country.

Leaving me far behind. I'm trying to be happy for her that she got a stupid scholarship to stupid Florida State to play stupid soccer, but it's not like they don't have soccer in Washington.

Three months of school, plus summer vacation, is not a lot of time to pack in four years' worth of sister-time. As terrifying as the Ridderlands were all those years ago, I wish we could have one last adventure together to remind her how much she needs me. Maybe then she'll change her mind. Maybe then she'll decide to stay.

Chapter Two

S ue B picks me up from school because today is Friday, and she promised we could spend time together without Hillary tagging along. We've got pizza money from Mom and Dad, our favorite playlist pulled up, and the rest of the night to do whatever we want.

I've been dropping hints all week that they have the best pizza at The Leaderboard. It's this retro gaming arcade that gives you a cup of these coin-like tokens that are supposed to be just like quarters to play the games. Dad says this is as close as you can get to the real thing without driving a long way off—or finding a time machine. Sue B always kicks my butt at Skee-Ball and electronic basketball, but she is awful at regular video games, even the ancient ones like Pac-Man and Galaga. Dad would cry if he heard me calling them old, but he's practically prehistoric himself.

I like hanging out with Sue B at the arcade because it's chaos in the best way and we're so busy she doesn't have time to check her phone—or even notice her phone going off.

"Wouldn't you rather go somewhere quiet where we can chat?" she says as I settle into the beat-up blue hatchback she calls "Cookie Monster." I always joke that the rust chunks falling off are the cookie crumbs.

"Sure, if I thought you'd pay attention to me the whole time."

"That's not fair, Jess. I've got a lot of stuff going on right now."

It's not like I don't believe her; she's gone through the list a bajillion times. Every time I complain about missing her. Travel soccer, yearbook committee, end-of-year testing, babysitting, her part-time job tutoring, and so many other things she didn't have to sign up for but insists she needed for her college applications and totally could have quit once she got accepted.

"You promised me today was just about me and you time, so we're going to The Leaderboard and eating greasy pizza and playing overpriced games for cheap-o prizes," I demand.

"You stole that line from Dad," Sue B accuses.

"I sounded just like him, didn't I?" I put my finger across my upper lip, copying his awful mustache.

"Eww, when is he going to shave that thing?"

In my best Dad voice, I repeat his practiced response to this common question. "What? It's growing on me." We suspect he only keeps it for the sake of the joke now. And I'm grateful for anything that gets my sister laughing these days.

I wiggle my finger off my lip and in her direction. "Oh no, now it's growing on you."

Sue B swats my mustache finger away as she fakes terror, but the car behind us in the pickup line honks to get us moving, and the game is over.

"To The Leaderboard," she says, putting Cookie Monster in drive. "I just have to make one quick call first."

Her "quick" call with Hillary wraps up right as we pull into the parking lot. So much for our playlist. Instead, I get to listen to twenty minutes worth of planning out their weekend in detail.

Not a second to waste, as Hillary likes to remind Sue B.

"Can we go in already?" I beg.

"We have all night, Jess. They're not going to run out of plastic spider rings and poorly-made stuffed animals. Give me one more minute to get myself organized, and I promise this is the last thing."

One minute becomes seven—yes, I'm timing her—but she finally gives me the thumbs up. I slam my body weight into the door, both because I'm annoyed and because it's the only way to open it from the inside.

"You could wait for me to let you out," Sue B digs.

But I'm sick of waiting around for her, so I step out and slam the door shut behind me, sending a few new "cookie crumbs" falling to the ground. "Sorry," I blurt.

Sue B responds with a glare. "You're lucky she only needs to last me until I leave for school."

She's smiling, but her words are like a punch straight to my stomach. "Don't remind me."

Sue B wraps an arm around my shoulders and gives a squeeze that's supposed to make me feel better about being abandoned.

As we walk out of the quiet parking lot and into the flashing lights and trilling noises of the building, Sue B pulls me aside. "Need to use the bathroom before we get started?"

I throw up my hands and roll my eyes. "Can you stop acting like such an adult for one night? *You* sound like *Mom*."

The punch to my shoulder tells me she gets the point. "Fine, I'll race you to the token machine, but first, tie your shoe."

I look down, and Sue B takes off. I'm wearing slip-ons. She's going to pay for that. By the time I catch up, she's already collecting tokens in the big paper cup they give you to carry them around. I love the clinking sound they make as they tumble in.

Despite the mixture of chiming, beeping, and ringing sounds all around us, the place is still pretty empty. We have our pick of any game in the place. Except Space Invaders. The owners' autistic son is obsessed with the game and is never not playing it. Rumor has it he's the reason they opened the arcade in the first place, which is a pretty cool parent move if you ask me. I can't even get my parents to buy me a karaoke machine, and no matter how hard I try, I can't get my old magic back to poof one into existence.

"Should I kick your butt in Skee-Ball now or later?" Sue B asks.

"Let's start with the most popular games before this place fills up," I suggest. "Then, we can take a break for pizza."

I don't usually like pinball that much, but I'm drawn to a game I've never seen before. The video display on the back panel is crazy lifelike, with asteroids falling from the sky and lava flowing around panicking dinosaurs. It's an extinction game where the pinball looks like a fireball and hitting the flippers deflects the ball away from killing various dinosaurs across the playing area.

"How about this one?" I ask.

Sue B rolls her eyes, already knowing she's going to lose. "Sure."

I let her go first, pretending to be kind, but actually wanting to see how it's played before I take my turn. She launches the ball using the electronic "pull" button instead of the old school manual kind, and the pinball goes flying over the digital display. As it spins, I'd swear there's real fire churning inside the ball.

She manages to bounce the pinball away from two dinos before missing a shot and watching it plummet to the bottom. When the ball disappears, the whole screen bursts into a flaming graphic, and I swear I can hear screaming coming from the game. I'm lost in the visual and noise.

Sue B shakes my shoulder and I finally look up. "I said it's your turn."

"Uh, let's play something else." I'm too disturbed to watch the dinosaurs die again. Maybe it's my connection to the ridders that makes it so creepy and realistic, but I don't like the way it makes me feel.

We play various games for about an hour and a half. It's enough to shake the terror from my head.

Sue B only sneaks a glance at her phone once. The combo of her competitive side and losing nearly every game is keeping her focused.

I'll see how she does while we're eating.

The pizza is hot, and the cheese is gooey. It's the perfect way to end the school week. While we wait for it to cool, I try to distract my sister from her phone so I don't lose her.

"You're having fun, right?"

"I'll be having a lot more fun now that we're done with first-person shooters and fighting games. Time for what I do best."

"Throw balls at things?" My question is teasing. "What a claim to fame."

"You won't be so sarcastic when I'm winning the World Cup," she retorts.

"I didn't know they had a championship in knocking clowns down with a ball."

Sue B kicks me under the table, then changes the subject. "I'm sorry we don't get to do this more often. Hillary and I—"

I make a gagging gesture and earn another kick.

"Hillary and I have worked really hard to qualify for as many scholarships to pay for college as possible. That means extra-curriculars and perfect grades. It's definitely not as much fun as hanging out with you, but someday you'll understand."

"Maybe, but you're accepted, and you got your scholarship. Shouldn't that mean you have more time now?"

"That's just not how it works. I'm working so I have money for the things I'll need at school, like books and food. If I let my grades slip or don't keep up with my training, I could lose my scholarship. Even if I'm not able to spend as much time with you as we'd like, you'll always be my sister. I'll always love you."

Sue B grabs my hand to comfort me, but I pull it away quickly and turn to wipe a tear that's ready to fall from my eye. When I look back at her, she's still got her eyebrows pulled together as she stares at me. I respond by taking a bite of the still-burning pizza and practically melting the skin on the roof of my mouth.

"S'good," I mumble with a thumbs up.

She relaxes her face and dabs the grease off her slice with a napkin.

Chapter Three

The place can get pretty packed on a Friday night, and today is no exception. By the time we finish our dinner, there are families waiting for tables. We clear our trays so someone else can take our spot and head back towards the gaming area.

That's when I see Barnaby. Here with a couple of guys from school. I almost don't recognize him. He's always been bigger than everyone around him, but now he blends in with the rest of the crowd. It must be a year or two since I've seen him. Don't get me wrong, he and Sue B are still friends, just not close like her and Hillary. He used to come over with his sister Ana sometimes when he and Sue B were still in middle school, but once they started at Plank Street High, we only ever ran into him at school events.

I think Sue B spots him too, except instead of heading over to say hi, she darts in the other direction, grabbing my hand to pull me along with her.

"What was that about?" I ask.

"What?"

"You're really going to play dumb? Both of us are too smart for that game," I say, calling her out.

With a grunt, she comes clean. "Fine. Things are a little…awkward between Barnaby and me right now."

"Is he picking on you again?" I'm ready to go smack him if he is.

"No, no, nothing like that. We're just not talking to each other at the moment. No big deal. Can we please get back to me making a fool of you at Skee-Ball?"

I raise an eyebrow at how sus she's being, but I can't ignore her challenge. "I'll have you know, Dad and I have been practicing while you and Hillary were busy picking up trash in the town parks and walking the elderly's dogs. Or is it elderly dogs? Whatever."

"You know," she says, "if you really want to spend more time with me, you can always join me for volunteer hours."

"No, thanks. I'm not that desperate. And if you say beggars can't be choosers, I'm going to call you Mom again."

"Rude," Sue B replies.

She inserts a token in each of our machines and the bell rings to signal the start of a game. As the balls tumble down into the gutter, I forget all about her and Barnaby and whatever is going on between them and focus on the job in front of me—beating Sue B for the first time ever in Skee-Ball.

Alarms go off. Sue B's first roll goes straight into the 100 hole, the hardest shot to make. I roll mine too hard, and it bounces off the back and falls down into the ten. I'll have to go faster and roll with more accuracy if I'm going to have a chance. Fifty, thirty, and fifty again. Meanwhile, Sue B's shots are nearly perfect. She's going to be relentless when I take the L. A few more throws and the chimes signal the end of the game and the beginning of my humiliation.

"I thought you said you practiced?" she asks.

"Who's being rude now?"

"Sorry," she says. "I shouldn't gloat after all the losing I did earlier, but it feels so good. Rematch?"

"Maybe I need to warm up first. Let's play something else for a while," I suggest. "What about…" I look around. "Air Hockey?"

"I can't believe it. Is Jessie Beezly backing down from a challenge?"

I'm about to launch into a major offensive when two strong arms come from behind and lift me into the air. I flail and kick until I'm set back down and swivel sharply to face my attacker.

"Whoa, Jessie Jess. It's me." Barnaby holds up his arms in surrender.

This prompts a snicker from his friends beside him that turns into full laughter when I glare at each of them in turn. "She's feisty."

Neither of us finds them very funny. In fact, Sue B has her arms crossed sternly over her chest, waiting for all of them to go away.

"Hey, guys, can you give me a minute?" asks Barnaby. Smart boy.

The group wanders off and Barnaby crouches down to my height. "How have you been, kid?" He's working really hard not to see my sister.

"I haven't been a kid for ages. And no one calls me Jessie Jess anymore." I wouldn't normally be so cold, but if Sue B is upset with him, I've got to have her back.

"Fair enough. I guess I haven't seen you in a while. I've missed you."

Maybe I'm seeing things, but I swear he just glanced over at Sue B.

"We've gotta get going, Jess," Sue B cuts in.

"But we—" I stop short, taking in my sister's expression. Her jaw is clenched, and speckled redness is flaring around her eyes. Something's really wrong. This isn't just a little fight between friends. "Oh yeah, I forgot Mom wanted us home early tonight."

Sue B turns away, and I grab her hand, still looking behind me. Where her face has tightened, his has fallen. He waves goodbye to me as Sue B drags me forward and out the front doors.

Chapter Four

After five straight minutes of silence, I can't take it anymore. "Are we going to talk about what just happened?"

"I have no idea what you're referring to," Sue B flat-out lies. "Unless you're talking about the part where you got destroyed in Skee-Ball. I remember that very well."

"Ha. Ha," I say without a drop of humor. "You don't need to tell me what happened between the two of you, but can you at least tell me if you're okay? Because you don't seem okay. And I just gave up another hour of game time *willingly* to get you out of there. That has to count for something."

"Thank you for doing that." She stops there, and I think I'm not going to get anything else out of her, but then she pulls the car over to the side of the road and puts on the blinking lights. "If I tell you, I don't want you to intervene in any way. No butting in and trying to solve my problem or threatening his life or anything. You need to promise."

She's looking at me like a puppy waiting to be forgiven, desperate for me to agree not to meddle. But as far as meddling in my sister's life goes, I'm basically the entire gang on Scooby Doo crammed into one person. Let's just say the ridders aren't the only things I've saved my sister from over the years.

I bite my lip as I fight off my every instinct. She wants to tell me, and this is the only way. "Fine, I agree."

"Say you promise."

"I promise," I say through gritted teeth. But my hesitation disappears when I see the first tears trickle down her cheeks. "What did he do, Sue B?"

She takes a few heavy breaths before beginning. "You know how prom is in May, coming up, and maybe you've seen videos on TikTok with these huge promposals?"

I nod without speaking so she'll go on.

I hear an audible gulp. "He…he…Friday before last, Barnaby did this big promposal thing where he dressed up as the school's lumberjack mascot with a soccer jersey and made this sign that said, 'Come with me to the ball?' with a soccer ball instead of the word ball. It was kind of perfect and embarrassing and cringe all at the same time."

"Wait," I interrupt. "Barnaby asked you to go to prom with him? Like, as his date?"

She nods and her face goes back to the sad puppy from before.

"And…you *wanted* to go with him?

Same sad puppy nod.

"So, what's the problem?" I'm lost.

"The promposal was meant for someone else. He asked me as a backup. He wanted to take Hillary instead, but she already had a date."

Her tears are pouring down her face now, and her nose is running. I've never seen my sister so upset over anything before. Not even when we were facing certain death at the hands of Mr. Ritter.

I dig through my backpack and hand her a wad of tissues from the bottom. When she's finished wiping away the snot, I reach over and give her a giant hug. We stay like this until the sniffles are nearly gone.

Once we're separated, I ask a lingering question. "How did you find out? Did he tell you?"

"His sister did."

"Ana came up to you?" It's usually not this hard to follow Sue B's stories.

"After school, I overheard her asking him how it went with Hillary."

"Maybe she was talking about something else?" I know, as I say it, that it's not true, but I can't think of anything else to say.

She shakes her head 'no' in the saddest way possible. "He tried to shush her, but it was too late. He saw the look on my face as they walked by my locker. If it had been about something else, wouldn't he have explained instead of rushing out of the building, dragging Ana behind him?"

What a moron! I think. *A reckless, stupid fool.*

"I'm really sorry he hurt you," I say. "You don't deserve to be someone's second choice. After all these years, Barnaby is delulu if he thinks Hillary is better than you."

"Hey, she's my best friend. This isn't her fault," Sue B defends. "It's not about wanting to be first. He should have planned something different for me. Not recycled his plan for Hillary. There's still two months before prom."

"Maybe he was worried someone else was going to ask you if he waited? You're pretty great." Of course, I'm trying to make her feel better, but this seems like a good explanation to me.

"Why are you defending him?" she snaps at me.

"Whoa! I'm not. He's the bad guy in this situation, I just don't think he's a *bad* guy, like in general. I don't think he'd hurt you on purpose, but he did hurt you. I'm one hundred on your side."

She doesn't respond. Instead, Sue B turns off her flashers and flicks her blinker to get back on the road.

Chapter Five

I admit, I thought last night would make Sue B see how much she misses hanging with me. A big ask for one night. But I never expected it to make things worse. How was I supposed to know that Barnaby would be there? Or that, after all these years, he'd hurt her like he used to? One thing that hasn't changed since I was little is that when something is going wrong in my sister's life, she always forgets we're on the same team, even though I'm her number one fan.

Now, I'm on her bad side even though all I did was suggest he might not have been thinking clearly. Basic common sense. If he was, he wouldn't have wanted to go with Hillary in the first place. *Duh*, Sue B.

She's in her room listening to breakup music as loud as Mom will let her and even canceled her plans with Hillary for the morning, claiming to have a headache. The lie to her bestie makes me think she never told Hillary what happened. Someone needs to do something, but I promised Sue B I wouldn't. It would be so easy to go to Barnaby's house and force him to apologize and fix his mess. Except teenage boys are dumb, and she'd know he didn't figure it out on his own, and she'd probably hate both of us even more than she does now.

I know she'll get over it eventually, and he'll either find the courage to face her, or they'll never speak again, but the longer it takes for that to happen, the longer it takes for me to get my sister back and make the most of the little time we have left together.

Too bad I can't lock them up together in a room until they work it out. That would definitely speed things up.

Rolling over on my bed, I open my bedside table drawer and pull out my Totoro notepad. It doesn't count as meddling if I don't get caught.

<u>Ways to get Barnaby and Sue B together without them knowing</u>
Trick Mom into inviting Plumbols for dinner
Ask Ana to help?
Have a teacher make them partners in class

These ideas suck. No one else is going to listen to me except maybe Ana, and isn't this partially her fault? She might not have known she was messing things up for my sister, but she did.

I shove the notepad back into the drawer after tearing the page out. Then, something in the back of the drawer catches under my fingernail. Using my thumbnail on the other hand, I pick it out. It's a piece of birdseed. Magic birdseed. The kind I thought I'd gotten rid of years ago. The kind that once took us back to the Ridderlands.

Sue B and Barnaby would have to work their problems out if we went there. They'd have no choice. That place has a way of making you face the things you've been hiding from. But it's really dangerous. We'd have to be dumb to go back a third time—except...

Except Ritter is gone, and it's *not* dangerous anymore. I made friends with the ridders last time we were there. They helped us defeat Ritter when he tricked Barnaby into being his friend.

Is it possible I could still communicate with them after all these years? If I called out to them, would they come?

This could be exactly what I've been looking for. I get all the time I want with Sue B, and she can work things out with Barnaby and go to prom when we get back. Plus, we'd have one last big adventure together. Maybe she'll even change her mind about Florida. She doesn't have to know I sent us there. In fact, she'll never forgive me if she finds out. But that's why it's so perfect. Sue B will never suspect me of something this crazy.

I haven't had magic for five years. I don't even know if it's possible to bring it back or talk to the ridders from the real world. And even if I manage to call out, maybe they left the Ridderlands behind after they tore Ritter apart. Found a better home with waterfalls and beautiful plants growing everywhere. I know I wouldn't want to live there forever. But I do want to visit one last time, and I need their help to do that.

Eyes closed, I concentrate as hard as I can, so hard my head shakes just like it did when I was little. Of course, nothing happens. I let out a laugh at the silliness. I'm almost as old as Sue B was the first time we traveled to that horrible world. She didn't have magic then; we thought she was too old. I'm probably too old now too.

"All right," I say to myself. "Enough pouting." I've never been a quitter. Jessie Beezly doesn't give up that easy.

My eyes close again, and I'm not just focusing, I'm believing. Isn't that what it used to take? Sue B and Barnaby had to believe in me for my magic to work. And now that I'm at the age where magic doesn't seem so real anymore, I'm going to believe in me myself.

Chapter Six

A whooshing sound passes between my ears, leaving me lightheaded. I'm not sure if I've concentrated too hard or if it's working, but it fizzles out too quickly for me to discover which it is. I really hope I'm not breaking my brain.

Come on, ridders, I call in my mind. *Anyone out there remember me? It's Jessie.*

All that appears is scribbly black and white like a marble notebook from writing class, only it's moving. Dancing around the screen inside my head.

Hello?

I imagine my magic pushing through the scribbles and reaching out towards the Ridderlands. But every time I get to what feels like the edge, I can't go any farther. There is something blocking me. A wall or a force field or something. When I was there before, I could simply think of what I wanted and it would appear: sandwiches, tea, my teddy bear. There's only resistance all around me now. Like my world isn't made for magic.

The single seed sitting on my side table catches my eye again. Somehow, all Sue B needed was a handful of the stuff to send a message to the ridders and call them to our world. One handful to be carried away, but all I have is one tiny seed. Maybe it's enough.

My hand squeezes the seed, though it's too small to even feel against my palm. The whooshing sound returns, and the pressure builds in my ears. I wait for the feeling to burst and fall away, but it intensifies. It's like being underwater in the deep end of the pool, diving to the bottom despite my body begging me to swim back to the top. The boundary is like the tiled pool floor, but it's no longer solid. This time, when I press against it, it gives a little. I keep pushing against the stretchy surface, willing it to break.

On the other side, I see it. The nearly-forgotten purple and blue swirling sky. The nests resting on cliff edges. But I also see tall grasses waving in a breeze along a winding river that I know was once nothing but dust and rocks.

I claw at the thin film separating me from the world I want to reach. It will not break. Did I come this far to be turned away?

Ridders!

I need your help to make it through.

Scanning the skies, I see no sign of them. They must have abandoned this place years ago. But why would they leave if their world is healing? Maybe they left too soon. They don't know it's changed.

Your home is beautiful again without Ritter. Can you hear me? Please come back and help me one last time!

A familiar screech echoes through their world and causes the film to vibrate. For a minute, I think the film will pop like a bubble and let me through, but the vibrations go away as the screeching fades.

It almost worked.

I want to try again. I know they're there this time, but my head is pounding. I need a break. My brain feels like I was trying to push it into a brick wall with no helmet. Something really doesn't want me to smash through. All that does is make me more determined to succeed. I'm Jessie Beezly, and I can do anything.

Chapter Seven

I can do anything except get my sister to come out of her room. For that, I need our mother. As much as Sue B and I tease her for being so annoying—like really annoying—without her, I wouldn't have this 'don't take no for an answer' attitude. It's kind of my favorite thing about me.

"Don't you think Sue B should eat something? She already missed breakfast."

Mom raises an eyebrow at me. "Your sister will come out when she's ready."

"So if your heart's broken, you can starve yourself?"

"Susan is not starving herself, nor is she heartbroken. You're being quite dramatic, Jessie." Mom's not taking the bait.

"*I'm being dramatic*? She's the one who locked herself in her room and won't talk to anyone." Mom gives me a 'watch your tone' look, and I consider giving up, but there has to be something I can say. I need to try a different way to get her interested. If there is one thing Mom can't stand, it's not having all the answers, all the details. "You know this whole thing is over Barnaby Plumbol, right?" Sue B will be so mad at me for telling.

"No, I didn't. But that's her business."

I nearly laugh, stopping myself in time to avoid a glare. Our business *is* Mom's business as long as we live in her house, or so I've heard her say when we try to keep secrets.

"You really don't want to know what's going on?" I ask her, pretending to be shocked. "You aren't curious at all what he did to her?"

Mom does one of those heavy huffs of breath out of her nose. I'm either getting to her, or I'm about to get yelled at.

"It's been a long time since she shed tears over that boy."

Yes! She's on the hook.

"I didn't know they still spent time together," Mom says.

"There are a lot of things we don't know about the two of them. She really didn't tell you about this whole messy problem?" I nudge her with the question. She's said a million times that a good mom knows what's going on with her kids.

Mom's only answer is a quiet "hmm" under her breath. She goes back to emptying the dishwasher, but I can see the change in her face. Little twitches in the mouth and eyes. I've got her worried and ready to barge in. I'm betting she's going through every possible scenario. From the simplest to the worst case.

I head back upstairs to get out of Mom's way and avoid being told to finish the dishes for her. I also want to listen in when Mom can't help herself and starts questioning Sue B.

It doesn't take long before I hear the slooshing of the dishwasher running, followed by the creaking of Mom's footsteps up the stairs. If Sue B didn't have her music so loud, she'd know what was coming for her. It's one of the tricks she taught me when I stopped being the cute baby and started getting into trouble. Count the creaks to know how close Mom is. This time, the creaks stop early. Then change. She's going back down. No. She stops again.

Why is she hesitating? This is a no-brainer for our mom. She's not a big fan of privacy—not ours—and her usual approach to moping is to put us to work. Why is Sue B getting special treatment this time?

I listen carefully for Mom to make up her mind. It's so quiet I can't tell if she's still there. Cautious to keep my own floor quiet, I lay flat on my stomach at the base of the door and press my ear to the space at the bottom. I'm lying like this awhile, the carpet fibers rubbing roughly against my cheek, making it itch, before Mom descends the rest of the way.

So much for that plan.

Chapter Eight

I'm swiveling in my desk chair and chewing my nails when Sue B's music suddenly cuts off and I freeze in place. Then, I hear her door open. Part of me wants to race into the hallway and make her listen to me, but I'm pretty sure she'll retreat. I don't have the patience to start the whole waiting thing over again.

For the second time today, I find myself face-down on the carpet and spying from the door gap. Only this time, I'm pressed right up against the door with one eye wedged in to see as far as I can while the other is squeezed shut. It's blurry, but I can just make out Sue B moving away toward the bathroom. I hope that's not the only reason she came out. She's in there a long time. I hear nose-blowing and the opening and closing of the cabinets and drawers. When the toilet flushes, I push in closer to my door. I can feel the deep groove forming across my forehead from its edge.

Sue B comes back toward her room but makes a turn at the landing and heads down the stairs instead. After the last stair creak, I can't tell where she goes, but I hear the mumble of her and Mom talking through the floor. It's not a long conversation. Definitely not Mom confronting her about everything that's going on, like I thought would happen—which is still super strange. Then the front door opens and closes, and Sue B is gone.

The whole house is extra quiet without her music thrumming. My ears feel stuffed up. It somehow makes missing her worse. Like all the Sue B has been sucked out of the world with a giant vacuum. She's told me before that it felt similar when she banished Barnaby and me to the Ridderlands. A void created where we should have been.

I roll away from the door and push myself up from my bedroom floor. A quick glance in the mirror shows I was right about the red, irritated line across my forehead from pressing at the door with my face. I try rubbing my palm against it to smooth it out, but it only makes the rest of my forehead red too. That'll take a while to fade.

Since there's no chance I can go ask Mom where Sue B went until it goes away on its own, what better use of my time than trying to reach the ridders again? I pull the tiny seed back out of my drawer and pinch it between two fingers. I want to feel it there as I imagine the Ridderlands and reach out to my giant flying friends. In my palm it was lost, but now it's a key, ready to be put in the lock and turned. Hopefully, it won't hurt my head as much as trying to bash my way in. My eyes close and I roll the seed against the tips of my thumb and pointer finger.

The magic tingles right away at the back of my neck. It's much stronger than my last attempts, and I didn't have to work for it at all. I open my eyes from the shock of it and the prickling fades away. Next time I'm ready for it. My eyes close, and the zing of magic brings every hair on my body to attention, like static electricity.

Instead of pushing straight for the swirling purple skies of the Ridderlands, I remember we always started from a dark, empty room. This is where the ridders would come to carry us away. It's plenty dark behind my closed eyes, but I imagine the darkness getting thicker like sludge or ink or tar. No tiny specks of light. Then I focus on the stuffy quietness from the absence of Sue B's music. There is no light or sound in this waiting room. When I think I have it perfect, I call out for the ridders, rolling the seed in my fingertips the whole time.

I know you're there. I know you hear me. I need your help.

If they come, there will be a slight breeze before I hear them approach. But there is only silence.

I don't know why you're ignoring me. I'm sorry I never reached out before. It's been a really long time. But I need you all now. Barnaby, Sue B, and I need you to come get us. I wouldn't ask if it wasn't an emergency.

The air pops with a screech so far away I can barely hear it. It's there, though. I almost open my eyes with the excitement that they're answering me. I need to stay focused so I don't lose the connection.

I hear you, I call back to them inside my head. *Please come for us now!*

This is no little breeze. A tornado of wind whips around and shoves me. It's much stronger than what I can remember. There's no question. They're coming. I can hardly believe it worked. All those years without magic, and now I can feel it buzzing in the air. Though I know what to expect, my teeth are chattering and my legs feel ready to give out. The ridders respond to my call with such a loud screech that I reach to cover my ears, but before my hands make it to my head, I'm ripped away into the sky and trying to get my breath to catch up with my body.

Chapter Nine

I'm so much bigger than the last time I went flying through this world. The heaviness of my body makes it scarier, like I could slip out of this ridder's grip at any moment, but I know she has me tight. Her long claws wrap all the way around my upper shoulders and under my armpits. Still, I find myself squeezing my eyes shut the whole time. Like that will stop me from falling.

Instead of the nest I'm expecting to be dropped into, the ridder sets me down gently on solid ground. The trickling sounds are what trigger me to open my eyes and see the new river flowing beside me.

"Where are we?" I ask aloud, even though they only speak inside of my head.

Much has changed. We are safe here, away from rocks.

In the distance, I see the familiar cliffs and plateaus. But there are hardly any nests, and those I see are broken or falling away.

"You left the nests behind?" I'm trying to make sense of what I see.

Rather than words, she responds with a screech. I'm about to ask her what she means when another ridder answers her call. That's when I see two others coming closer, carrying Sue B and Barnaby with them.

"You're amazing! You got them here."

My debt is now paid.

There isn't time to figure out what that means before something else draws my focus. I'm beaming up at my sister, but the look on her face isn't a happy one. Her nose is wrinkled up and her eyes are like weapons. I've seen this face a million times over the years. She's going to kill me. Maybe for real this time. I shift my smile over to Barnaby, hoping for a happier reunion, but no such luck. He's not as murderous as Sue B, but his face looks as white as snow and a little melty.

Once they're on land, the ridders release them from their grips and take off without so much as a goodbye. Nothing is like I expected.

"What the hell is going on, Jessie?" Sue B shouts her question at me.

If the ridders aren't sticking around, then no one else knows I'm responsible for bringing us here—not that my sister speaks ridder anyway. Sue B can thank me later when she's figured out what a genius I am for solving her problems. For now, she doesn't need to know I'm behind our unexpected adventure.

"I'm just as confused as you are. But I'm happy to see you guys. I thought I was going to be here alone."

"How long have you been waiting?" asks Barnaby.

"I'm...uhh...not sure. Have you two seen all the changes?"

"I've been trying my best *not* to think of this place for the last five years. I don't want to notice changes. I want to close my eyes and go back to pretending this whole world doesn't exist," my sister yells.

Sue B is crashing out, and I don't understand why. It's not like we're being threatened right now. The ridders are on our side—at least I thought they were before the whole 'debt paid' thing—and the Ridderlands don't even look scary anymore. The swirling purple sky is still dark, but the river is pretty, and there are real plants and grasses and stuff growing around here. I think I even see some flowers.

"You do remember that we got rid of Ritter, right? There's nothing here to hurt us anymore," I remind her.

"Stop being so childish. This isn't some kind of playland, Jessie. Being here hurts the people at home who forget about us. Not to mention, we're never brought here for good reasons. We should all be freaking out," Sue B says.

"What about you, Barnaby?" I ask. "You've barely said anything."

"Sorry, kiddo. I'm with your sister on this one." He looks over at Sue B like he's waiting for a cookie.

She must not be in a forgiving mood yet because she crosses her arms and turns away from him. He may still be in the doghouse now, but by the end of this trip, everything will be happy again.

"We've beaten this place twice, with Ritter. This should be a piece of cake. No bad guy. No hungry ridders. We need to figure out what we're here to fix and head home."

"How do you know there's something here to fix, Jessie? There's nothing to fix. Everything is really, really great." Sue B's voice is hard and angry and defiant.

"Oh yeah. You sound like you're happier than you've ever been," I say sarcastically.

Sue B turns her weapon-eyes back on me and then re-aims at Barnaby before stomping off.

Before I follow after her, I grab Barnaby's arm. "Aren't you even going to try to apologize? Or do you plan to be useless the whole time?" Then I storm off too.

Chapter Ten

"Where are you going?" I ask as I catch up with Sue B. "Someone has to take charge and get us out of here. You used to speak their language; did the ridders tell you anything?" Her question catches me off guard.

"I—don't think I have my magic anymore."

"Oh great," she says, "now we're going to starve out here too."

Barnaby comes jogging up. "Now that there's plant life, some of this might be edible."

"Thanks, Boy Scout." Sue B definitely doesn't mean that thanks.

"Just trying to be helpful." Again, like a 'very good boy.'

I roll my eyes, making sure he can see. "We may not know what brought us back here this time, but I can say for sure that we're not going to get home with the two of you acting like this."

"I'll act however I want," growls Sue B. "This isn't my fault."

"Maybe if you would just tell me why you're so mad at—" Before Barnaby can finish, there's a crashing sound like thunder that roars through the sky.

"What the heck was that?" I ask.

Sue B freezes. "This isn't happening again. If I close my eyes, I'll see that I'm really home." She curls in a ball on the ground and wraps her arms tightly around her head like we do in lockdown drills.

Oh, crud. I broke my sister.

"It's going to be fine, Sue B. Probably just a thunderstorm. If there's a river here now, that means there has to be rain too, right? Any second, the drops will start falling. You'll see."

And something does start falling, but it's not raindrops. It's rocks the size of pebbles falling down like hail.

"We have to get under cover," Barnaby yells through the pinging sounds of rocks hitting everything. He grabs Sue B by the shoulders and heaves her up to her feet. "Come on! You can hate me just as easily from over there." He points to a tree with thick foliage.

"What if it lightnings?" I ask.

"Do you see any better options?"

He's right. There's nothing else around us we can shelter under. No caves, no overhangs. I grab Sue B's hand and pull her to the safest safety we have for now.

Didn't the ridder tell me I was safe here by the river, away from rocks? Why didn't she mention that the rocks could fall from the sky? Seems like the kind of thing you tell someone before you abandon them. Especially someone who was once a friend.

A bolt of lightning brighter than any I've ever seen pierces the dark sky.

"Crap, crap, crap. We have to get away from this tree," Sue B pleads, having finally rejoined us in reality.

"I have an idea," says Barnaby, and he pulls off his hoodie.

"How exactly does undressing help us?" I ask.

"If we all huddle together underneath my sweatshirt, it'll act as an umbrella and keep the majority of pebbles from hitting us directly. Then we can search for somewhere safer to take refuge," he explains.

"I'd rather get struck by lightning or pelted with stones than get that close to you," Sue B says dramatically.

"Have you completely lost your mind?" I respond. "Safety first, then you can go back to holding your grudge."

Barnaby reaches out a corner of his hoodie for Sue B to take with big shiny anime eyes.

I wedge between them. "I'll be the buffer since I'm not tall enough to hold it up anyway."

Reluctantly, Sue B takes the back two corners and spreads them over us like a tent. Barnaby does the same with the shoulders. We creep out carefully from the cover of the tree. A few pebbles ricochet off their legs, but I'm pretty safe in the middle. I don't see anywhere else to shelter, so we walk slowly without a solid direction to go in.

The sky looks intense when the lightning crackles through the swirls and lights up the falling rocks all around us. With every deafening bang, there are more and more stones falling. It's as if someone has a hammer in the sky and is smashing some great boulder into bits. Not the most comforting vision to have right now.

"Does anyone see anywhere we can go?" I ask, suddenly more concerned than before.

"What's that over there?" Barnaby asks.

"I don't see anything? Over where?" Fear must be setting in because Sue B's voice has less sting to it now.

"Farther down the riverbank. It's a hole of some kind. Looks deep enough to climb into."

"And that helps us how?" I ask. "Holes don't have roofs."

"We'll still need to use my shirt to cover overhead, but at least it'll protect us from the sides, and we shouldn't be at risk from the lightning."

There doesn't appear to be any other option, so I agree. "Better than standing in the open."

We have to sit scrunched up in order to fit inside. I'm sure Sue B isn't happy to be trapped like this with two people she doesn't want to talk to. Luckily for her, the weird storm lets up within an hour of our uncomfortable silence. It comes as no surprise that she's the first to climb out of the hole.

Chapter Eleven

As the last of the pebbles ping off the ground, Barnaby helps me out of the hole. Sue B is standing close by, staring out across the river toward the mountains and cliffs. Her left hand covers her mouth, and her eyes are wide.

"What are you looking at?" I ask. "You're freaking me out."

She doesn't answer. Instead, she points where she wants me to look. Back across the river is a series of holes zig-zagging into the distance, though I only see the tops.

"More holes?"

"Not holes," corrects Barnaby. "Footprints. Really big footprints."

I still don't see what they're seeing. I can't believe I'm about to ask this, but I hate feeling left out. "Can you pick me up so I can see?"

"Sure thing, kiddo."

I ball my fists at this new childish nickname but bite my tongue before yelling at him. I can't expect them to get along if I'm starting fights myself.

Barnaby lifts me up uncomfortably by my armpits—which are still tender from the ridder-ride in—and places me up on his shoulders like I weigh nothing. Now that I have a height advantage, I see what they mean. The holes alternate like footsteps. They're not really foot-shaped, but I can't think of how else they might have gotten here.

"Why do they stop with this one foot over the river?" I press my hands onto Barnaby's shoulders as I slide off his back to closely examine the hole we just came from.

"She's right," says Sue B. "There aren't any other holes that I can see on this side of the river."

"Honestly, I'm less concerned with why it stopped than what it is. Whatever made these holes had to be huge and heavy," notes Barnaby.

"Heavy like rock?" The question comes out with a shiver.

I keep coming back to what the ridder said to me, '*We are safe here, away from rocks.*' Since when have the rocks been dangerous? And the ridder said '*We.*' Does that mean they're scared of the rocks? That could be why they abandoned their nests, why they took off so quickly once we got here. There's too much I don't understand and no one to help me figure it out. If I tell my sister I lied about the ridder talking to me, she'll want to know why I didn't tell her in the first place.

"You mean like falling boulders?" Barnaby asks. "That wouldn't explain the walking pattern they'd need to have landed in or the fact that there are no boulders in those holes."

"Duh. Obviously, it's not boulders."

"Some things never change," he complains.

"If not boulders, then what?" Sue B prods.

"I don't know," I yell. "Why do I have to have all the answers? I'm ten."

Sue B lets out a drawn-out grunt of frustration. "Maybe you shouldn't act like you know everything then. Not every problem is something you can whisk away."

"Funny coming from you," snips Barnaby.

"Seriously?! How can you possibly still be mad at me about something that happened in sixth grade? Wait a minute! Is that why you embarrassed me by asking me to prom with Hillary's promposal? Some kind of payback?" I see the tears welling up in her eyes, and her cheeks are speckled red.

Barnaby has gone ghost white again. "I asked you to prom because I wanted to go with you. Because I like you, Sue B. I have for a long time."

"You just like Hillary more," she replies bitterly.

Their fight is so intense I almost don't notice the shaking of the ground beneath us. Tremble and pause, tremble and pause.

"Hey, guys," I interrupt.

"What?" they both snap simultaneously.

I don't have to explain because the next tremble is stronger and nearly knocks the unsuspecting Sue B over.

"I'm glad you're finally talking, but we've got bigger problems than prom. Like much bigger."

Chapter Twelve

The trembling becomes full-on quaking as we search the landscape for some sign of what's causing it and where it's coming from. Staying upright is almost impossible, but we still don't see anything.

"How are we supposed to hide from something we don't see?" I plead. The next vibration sends me down to my right knee hard, and I howl in pain. Barnaby races over unsteadily and rips the hem from his hoodie to tie around my knee and stop the blood that's now dripping down my leg and pooling in my sock.

"We've got two options. We can find somewhere to hide, or we can run as far away from these mountains as possible," he says while tightening the knot.

"Ow. What do we do, Sue B?" I need my sister's big brain to get us out of this.

"Just let me think for a minute." In obvious distress, she covers her ears with her hands again. "I can't think with all this pounding and shaking and blood."

"We don't have—"

"Shh," I silence Barnaby.

"Okay," Sue B says, settling herself, "if we hide, this side of the river seems the safest, and there isn't much but trees and tall grasses. Nothing that will protect us from being squished by whatever's coming. But if we run, we could be going in the opposite direction of wherever we need to go to get out of here. We haven't been here long enough to discover our objective or dream up a solution—if that's even possible without Jessie's magic."

I turn my eyes away at hearing my dangerous lie taken for truth.

She continues. "Hiding could give us a chance to see what we're up against, especially if we have to face it at some point. Running gives us a better chance of survival but could leave us trapped here forever and erase the futures we've been working so hard toward."

That last bit tells me why she's so freaked out this time around in a way she hasn't been since she was young. Sue B is normally way more confident than this. She'd have an answer for us already.

Barnaby looks at me with flared eyes. I widen mine right back at him in challenge. Why do I have to be the one to push her further? Probably because I'm her sister and she sort of hates him right now.

"You've broken it down. What's the answer, sis?"

"Running away has never solved our problems here. There's always some challenge to face, some hurdle to clear. Let's hide." Sue B nods with certainty.

Without asking, Barnaby lifts me up like he's about to rock me to sleep and takes off running toward a grouping of trees half a football field away. He doesn't even bother to see if Sue B is following, but I hear her feet thudding behind us in the pauses between the thunderous quakes.

When we reach the trees, Barnaby sets me down on the grass behind a tree trunk and only then turns to find my sister. Is he upset with her, or does he trust her to make it on her own?

"Remember the first time we were here?" I ask Sue B. "You two hated each other, but you knew Barnaby was strong enough to carry me and run so we could all get away. I guess things haven't changed as much as I thought."

"Your sister is the best at basically everything else, but I'll always be bigger."

For a moment, they forget they're fighting and in danger, and they share a laugh. "You're more than just big," Sue B says quietly. I don't know if he even hears her. She comes to my side and fiddles with the quickly made wrap covering my knee gash, undoing it and rewrapping the wound until she's satisfied with the results. First aid is another activity she did for her college apps.

"Do you see what's causing the tremors, Barnaby?" I'm hoping he's chosen a spot that's far enough away to be safe but close enough to spy on whatever it is.

"I wish we had our backpacks full of supplies. Some binoculars would be really useful right about now. The rock formations seem to be changing, but I don't see anything actually moving."

"That makes no sense."

"Duh, Jessie." Barnaby lets out a blast of laughter. "I've been waiting a really long time to say that back to you."

Even Sue B has a chuckle at that.

"Focus," I remind them. "What do you mean the rocks are changing?"

"At first, it was only a nest falling off the edge of a cliff up there on the left. I figure that could happen from all the vibrations and whatnot, right?"

"Right," Sue B confirms.

"But then a new opening appeared between the two high points in the center. It seemed like one solid mountain before. Now it's definitely split in two, yet there are no signs of a collapse. Like the middle of that mountain just got up and left."

Sue B and I look at each other with major eek face.

"Hold on," his voice rises.

"What?" I urge.

Barnaby stands up and leans forward from behind the tree trunk where he hides. "You have to see this!" He waves us over hurriedly.

My sister helps me up, and we both peek around opposite sides of our hiding place. "Where are we looking?" she asks.

"Just wait for it. You'll see."

I hold my breath as my eyes dart back and forth, looking for any sign of movement. As my chest tightens, my eyes grow wider, trying to take in every centimeter so I won't miss a thing. Still, nothing happens. Not even a falling nest or rockslide. In fact, the quakes have stopped too. I empty my lungs and go back to breathing normally. Either it didn't happen, or whatever it was isn't going to happen again.

My weight shifts onto my good leg so I can lean against the trunk and slide down into a more comfortable sitting position once more. But the minute I take my eyes off the sky, Sue B squeals with a sharp inhale. I'm fast enough to catch the end. A huge chunk of rock explodes like a firework. The falling pieces splash into the river below. Within minutes, another boulder comes flying toward us out of the mountains, bursting at the river line again. All that speed and not a single shard of schist or grain of granite makes it more than 100 feet past the river.

"Why do they explode when they reach the water?" I ask.

"What do you mean? They aren't landing in the river." I'm tempted to give Barnaby a deserved 'duh,' but what I have to say is too important.

"Look where the boulder is in the sky when it bursts."

Another ginormous hunk goes flying in our direction. Sue B is the first to look at me with that smile that means she's figured it out. "As soon as the mass makes its way directly above the river's border, the rock shatters like it's hit a wall or force field or something."

"So we're safe as long as we're far enough away, but who or what is hurling mountains at us?" As excited as I am to solve a piece of the puzzle, Barnaby is right. Something is trying to harm us, and with Ritter out of the picture, we have no idea who we're dealing with.

Chapter Thirteen

"We have good reason to believe we're safe where we are, right? So we stay here, plan, get some rest, and tomorrow we figure out what's going on with the mountains. Sound fair?" Sue B asks.

"Fair enough," replies Barnaby.

I nod. My knee is throbbing with pain, though there's no swelling, which I assume is a good thing. "Can I use your hoodie to elevate my knee if you're not gonna put it back on?" Barnaby tosses it over to me, and I arrange myself in a more comfortable position in the plush grasses a few feet away from him and Sue B. Fingers crossed, they'll take the opportunity to talk.

Everyone is quiet for the longest time. Barnaby stares into the distance, watching the mountains. Sue B plays with her car keys and steals glances at him when she thinks no one is looking. I've never seen two people so afraid to talk to one another. Maybe they need a nudge.

"Do you think we'll have dreams?" I ask, drawing both of their attention.

"I hope so," Barnaby says. "We've never done this without your magic. Even when Ritter pretended to be JR and blocked you from using it, the magic saved us in the end."

"Are you sure you don't feel it at all?" Sue B presses.

I could claim it's coming back to me, work around my lie and give them some hope, but they aren't much closer to fixing things between them than they were this morning. They need to do this part themselves. "I'm sure."

Sue B digs around in her crossbody bag that she must have been wearing when she was taken and pulls out a granola bar. "Wanna split it?" she asks. Barnaby and I nod, and she breaks it into thirds and passes it around.

We all return to our silence.

The sky gradually takes on darker shades of purples and blues. As I stare up into the swirls and stars, it hits me how different this place feels from when I was younger. It used to feel like a storybook. I felt so certain I was the hero, and even when I was terrified, like when we were attacked by the watchers, I somehow knew we'd get to the happily ever after. That's how all the stories ended. But there is a heck of a lot of life that happens after that point. People grow up, maybe even grow apart. People take on different meanings in our lives. Nothing stays the same forever, no matter how much you want it to.

Everything feels realer this time. We aren't playing a game or stuck in a fairytale. Bad things could happen here. We could lose. I thought we'd be safe with Ritter gone, but maybe there's another bad guy trying to take the most important things away from me.

I'm the one who wanted this adventure, and as Mom would say, I bit off more than I could chew. Dad would say I got more than I bargained for. Both of those are overly complicated ways of saying I got my wish and now I regret it.

Is it really my fault if the mountains themselves have risen up to take over the Ridderlands with the ridders gone? I don't think so.

Sure, I could have been less impulsive—Mom's favorite word to describe me—and given the whole plan more than a few hours to come together, but problems require action, not just sitting around and crying about things while you wait for someone else to do the hard stuff for you.

Sue B was ruining everything I've tried so hard to protect. I might be the one that comes to her rescue, but I need my big sister around. She covers for me when Mom is doing too much, gets me out of the house if our parents have one of their rare but intense fights, and takes care of me if they both have to work late. I'm not ready to handle those things on my own yet. I'm not even allowed to be home alone.

Two days ago, it didn't matter if Sue B still talked to Barnaby. I didn't even know if they were friends anymore. At the arcade, he came storming back into my life, and I realized I missed him. All three of us are connected forever by this place and what we've been through. When I found the seed in my drawer, it seemed so perfect that the Ridderlands were there to bring us all together again.

Maybe it wasn't my idea at all.

Chapter Fourteen

I'm at the top of a cliff with lightning breaking the sky into a million jagged pieces. Below me, the stone is illuminated with each bright flash, showing the textures and colors on the sides of the rock walls. There is movement and shifting as figures emerge from cliff faces. They disappear in the darkness and shadows only to appear again in another spot when the lightning casts a glow over everything.

I know I should be scared. They are huge and seem indestructible. Men made of stone, much bigger than me, stronger than Barnaby. But instead of running, I stare them down. This is the battle we've come to face. This is why the world wanted me here.

My eyes open, and I see dancing leaves above me as the stars shine through the gaps. I'm covered in sweat, and my heart is racing. Maybe I was brave in the dream. Right now, I feel anything but. I shake out my arms to rid myself of the trembling in my hands. I know we're safe for now, but we won't be for long. I consider waking Sue B and Barnaby up to warn them, though I know they might be having their own important dreams. We need all the clues we can get if we're going to overcome these new rock monsters.

I'm tired enough that falling back to sleep shouldn't be this hard, but my knee still hurts, and the panic of my dream is making my body antsy. And I'm thirsty. My tongue is sticking to the roof of my mouth, and my lips are rough and crackly. I need to get a drink.

A bottle of water seems worth the risk of using magic so close to Barnaby and Sue B. Besides, if there is one thing I know about teenagers, it's that they love sleep. Mom is always reminding my sister she'll need to get up early for class and practice on her own next year and can't keep sleeping through her alarm clock.

If the magic is going to work, I'll need the seed. Wait! My mind flashes back to my bedroom, me rolling the seed in my fingers. But I don't have any memory of the seed after that. Did I drop it when I entered the waiting space? Did the ridder eat it as her payment for taking me? This is not good.

I close my eyes to try the magic anyway, though I don't feel confident. It almost worked without the seed earlier.

Water, water, water, water, water...

I repeat it over and over. Nothing shimmers or shakes or gives me goosebumps.

Can I have some water, please?

Of course, no one answers. Not the ridders or my magic powers. I guess I'm walking to the river.

It's not easy to get myself up from the ground. My habit is to push up on my right knee. I try that and bite my lip to keep myself from howling out in pain and waking them up. Rolling to the left instead, I'm able to get into a sort of crawling position, except I avoid putting my other knee down. From there, I straighten my left leg and bear crawl closer to the tree. Then I use it to pull up until I'm standing. Finally. Being injured sucks.

I scan the sky for exploding boulders. Everything is calm. I just need to get down to the river for a drink of water and back without getting hit with any shattering rocks. Simpler thinking it than doing it. Especially when I can't run as fast as I normally would if something goes wrong. Stupid knee.

I don't know if I can do this. Maybe I *should* wake up Barnaby. He wouldn't be mad at me if I did. Neither would my sister, even if they are both in the middle of important, necessary dreams.

No. *There's nothing to be scared of right now*, I tell myself. I'm going.

I hobble toward the river. Hobbling is the perfect word to describe the way I'm walking as I try not to put any weight on my right leg. Who knew one knee was so important to how my body moves? I don't take a straight path in order to make myself a moving target. Instead, I zigzag from grass to tree or bush. Honestly, I'm not sure if I don't want to get there or if I'm being really smart about it. Either way, it might take me the rest of my life to make it.

I'm being dramatic, which is not my style. This is seriously taking forever, though. I need to go straight across and get water before I die of thirst.

The rest of the walk is so boring it makes me feel stupid for worrying so much. I dip my hands into the clear, flowing water and pull it to my mouth. It's the most delicious water I've ever tasted, cold and clean. After drinking so much, it makes my belly slosh like a jug, I get an idea. The wrap on my leg is crusty with dry blood, and so stiff it hurts to remove it. There's a bit of swelling that wasn't there before from walking on it. Once the wrap is off, I remove my socks and shoes as well and dangle my legs down into the drop-off of the water, turning slightly so my right knee goes completely under. The cold stings at first, but eventually the pain fades away. It's as if I never hurt it in the first place.

Is the river *magic*? I lift my leg, hopeful for what I'll see and…lower it back down in disappointment. The river is not magic. It's just cold and refreshing and normal, numbing the pain like an ice pack.

"You shouldn't have left without waking one of us up." Sue B's voice catches me by surprise and I bang my knee into the river's bank.

"Ouch."

I turn, expecting Barnaby too, but it's just her.

"You're not going to be around forever." I don't know why I say it—start a fight. It just comes out. Might as well do this. "I'm going to be doing a lot of things by myself from now on."

"That's true," she answers, way calmer than I expect her to be. "It's going to be hard for me to accept that."

"What do you mean?"

"Ever since you were born, I've been watching out for you. Not always because I wanted to, but most of the time I've really enjoyed being your big sister. Soon, I'll be going away to college, and everything is going to change."

"So don't go. If you don't want it to be different, then you can stay home and go to college here," I say. How can she be telling me this for the first time?

"It's not that easy, Jessie. It's really scary to grow up and leave home. But that doesn't mean it's not what's best for me. It might be what's best for you too."

"Best for me?" I'm in shock. "How is being left behind for the best? How is losing my sister who is supposed to be there for me *forever* for the best?" She's lost her mind if she thinks I'm going to believe a word of this.

"Jessie, please don't say that. You're not losing me. It's going to be very different for both of us, but I'll only be a phone call away whenever you need me. It's time that you focused on your own life now and less on me."

"What's wrong with my life?" Now she's being rude.

"Honest question, who's your best friend?" she asks.

"Y—"

"And don't say me."

"Well, it's true."

"That's a problem, Jessie. You need friends your own age. You need your own interests and hobbies."

Ouch.

"People respect me," I counter.

"Sure, but do they invite you to sleepovers? Birthday parties?" I can't answer her question the way I'd like to, and she knows it. "For years, you've been so focused on my life and solving all my problems that you didn't even consider you were missing out on making your own." Her words sting worse than the gash on my knee.

Is she right?

"How's the water taste?" Barnaby has somehow snuck up on both of us while we're busy arguing.

Part of me wants to tell him to go away so we can finish our conversation, but the other—much bigger—part of me is glad for the change of subject.

"It's good," I answer him, giving in to the easy option. "Really good."

Chapter Fifteen

S ue B glares laser beams at him, but Barnaby must assume it's just her continued anger over prom because he doesn't take her hint. Good. She's leaving for school, so I don't need her approval of my life. There are people who like me, even if we only see each other at school. It's not like I sit alone at lunch or hide in the bathroom like she used to. Sue B's not exactly an expert on friends. This whole promposal mix-up with Hillary proves it.

And aren't we here to fix their problem anyway?

The two of them drink in silence on opposite sides of me while I soak my knee. Maybe if Sue B wasn't so completely incapable of managing her own life, I wouldn't have to spend so much time focused on her instead of myself.

"So, what are you two going to do about prom?" My question lands like a grenade on the shore of this river. I flutter my eyelashes innocently, knowing full well I'm retaliating. Barnaby chokes on his water and ends up in a coughing fit while Sue B looks like she swallowed a fish whole and it's having trouble wriggling its way down into her stomach.

When Barnaby gathers himself enough to stop coughing, he looks sideways toward my sister to see what she'll do. As usual, she's gotten in her own way of solving whatever problem she has. It's obvious to me that he wants to resolve things and get back on her good side.

I get an idea that will both freak Sue B out and put her on the spot with him.

"I'll give you guys some space to talk things over." Without waiting for a response, I dive into the chilly river fully clothed.

The water bites at my skin and tenses my muscles, but it isn't rapid, and the river isn't wide, so swimming to the other shore won't be hard. I didn't take four years of swimming lessons in the summer for nothing. As I freestyle across, I hear Sue B yelling her disapproval every time I turn my head to take a breath.

Sorry, can't hear you. Busy with my own life, I think.

The shoreline on this side is a gradual slope rather than the big dropoff where I left Sue B and Barnaby behind, and I pull myself by my arms to land while my injured leg floats in the shallow water. I hope the cold has numbed the knee enough that standing will be easy because I don't want to have made a big show of my independence in front of Sue B only to flop around trying to stand up, then wibble-wobble away. I need this dub.

I turn over so I'm sitting in the silt and wring out the excess water from my short curly hair. It'll probably look like a big puffball after this stunt, but it's worth it if my sister apologizes. When my hair isn't dripping anymore, I get to work squeezing my t-shirt. Thank goodness I took my sneakers and socks off before—before I left them on the other side of the river with Sue B like a complete idiot.

Whatever, I'm a wild girl. I don't need any shoes.

I take my first look at the two of them watching me, stupefied.

"What do you think you're doing?" she asks.

"Focusing on me," I answer. No hesitation. No looking away.

"Should I go after her?" Barnaby's question goes ignored by both of us.

"I didn't mean doing any stupid little thing that comes to mind when I said that."

Now I'm friendless and stupid? I'm done talking to her. I totally ignore the shooting pain that pulses from my knee as I stand up quickly and walk down the shoreline away from them.

"Where are you going?" she shouts. "Get your butt back here." When I don't turn around or answer, I hear her say to Barnaby, "What are you waiting for?"

Then there's a splash.

Chapter Sixteen

I risk a quick look over my shoulder to see how fast Barnaby is coming while trying not to slow my wobble down. What I see catches me by surprise. Both Barnaby and Sue B are in the water, and my sister is splashing frantically as he tries to keep her above water. She manages to slap him across the face, and he lets her slip under once more.

Should I rush back? I freeze instead. I always assumed Sue B didn't take swim lessons with me because she learned to swim before I was old enough to remember; isn't it normal for teenage girls to always stick to floating on rafts? Now I'm wondering if she's been afraid of swimming her whole life. I should have known this. I should have taught her.

I take a step back toward them, but I stop myself. Barnaby will save her. He's more than capable. Didn't she tell me to stop worrying about her? Besides, I'm already injured and not big enough to be much help. I'd just be in the way, and we'd all end up drowning. As hard as it is to walk away from my sister in danger, that's exactly what I do. This is my opportunity to sneak away while they're distracted. Then Sue B can worry about me for once.

My walk turns into a hop-step, which is nearly a run, and I head farther down toward a bend in the river where I know they won't be able to see me. Once I make it around the turn, I lean against the edge of a rock formation to catch my breath and listen for my pursuers. There's no more splashing. Barnaby is telling Sue B to cough it out. She must be okay. My shoulders loosen a bit at the good news. Ignoring my sister while she's struggling is the hardest thing in the world for me to do.

Keep moving, I remind myself as a shiver creeps up my spine from the cold, wet clothes I'm wearing. Not only do I need to create some distance between me and them and warm myself up with movement, but it might be dangerous to stay in one place this close to a rock. I'm not on the safe side of the river anymore.

With my attention focused back on the path ahead of me, I see a glint of something shining not too far ahead. It's the first non-rock thing I'm seeing on this side, so I set the shiny spot as my target. Here I come, mysteriously twinkling object ahead. The path becomes more and more rocky as I move through, making me majorly regret forgetting my sneakers. Big fail. I head closer to the water line, hoping for a smoother walking surface and get lucky. The silt and sand are soft, fine-grained. I scrunch my toes in the grit and cool water that sloshes up around my ankles. If I close my eyes, I can almost pretend it's a day at the beach. Almost. There's still the threat that a rock could be hurled at me any minute.

Why do I do these things? This time, I literally jumped in without thinking—jumped in, swam across into danger, and ran away from the people who could help me.

My progress is much faster on the softer land. The closer I get to the shimmering, the bigger it gets. I thought it was something small, like when you see a piece of pyrite on a hike, and your heart jumps thinking you might have found gold. But this is a wall of darkness with a glinting light that bounces from spot to spot. I can't tell if the whole thing is reflective or if the reflective thing is moving around the black wall. The second option sends a shiver through my whole body, worse than from the cold. I slow my pace in reaction.

Maybe I should stop altogether and reconsider what I'm doing before

I make another big mistake, except I can't. As scared as I am, there's this feeling inside me that I need to find out what it is.

This world is strange. There are parts of it that want to trap us—even kill us—and other times it seems to want to help. The magic that got us home the first two times we came here had to come from somewhere in this place, and the world would quake to show us we were doing the right thing. I don't know if I'm heading for danger or safety, but I wish I had my sister with me.

Chapter Seventeen

A sheer wall of what looks like black ice stands before me, pressed up against the edge of the shoreline that goes on for miles. The whole surface is as reflective as a mirror, though, thanks to the dull light of the Ridderlands and the black color, my reflection looks as if I'm hiding in shadows. There are a few spots where the light catches the material just right and it gives off a reddish-brown tone inside. I've never seen anything like it.

When I press my hand against it, it's smooth and hard like glass. I pull my hand away, and it leaves a smudge and a steamy outline of my handprint on the cool exterior. Then something moves beneath the surface of the black mirror. Something I can't make out from where I stand.

I shimmy sideways along its front, feet in the water, as there is no dry shore to walk along here. Whatever is inside this massive wall is moving away from me, and I can't help but follow. When the movement stops, I've edged so far along that I can no longer see the place where the wall begins behind me.

WHAM!

Something slams against the surface from the inside, right in front of me, and I fly backwards, landing with a splash on the river's edge. When I look up, I gaze into my own eyes. A reflection of me stares down from inside the glass.

"Wh—How—" The words catch in my throat.

I stand back up and approach the wall cautiously. My reflection reaches forward like it wants to touch hands. So that's what I do, without thinking. Extending my left arm, I place my palm on theirs, and the exterior is no longer cool to the touch; I can feel their warmth—my warmth.

"Are you me?" I ask. My eyes are glued to the image before me.

It doesn't respond. Instead, it moves away.

"Wait! Don't go."

My reflection doesn't listen. Its right hand beckons me to follow as it moves farther and farther down the wall. So I follow, without a second thought. Another twenty feet down the length of the surface, and it stops and turns its back to me. We're both staring in the same direction at a bulletin board. The kind they post things on in the hallways at school for announcements, rosters, applications. In the center, there is a sign-up sheet for after-school clubs. Before my eyes, other students appear and swarm the list, writing their names under the ones that interest them. I read the club names but only take notice of which ones Sue B once belonged to: chorus, intramural soccer, 3D art club. Maybe I should register for one of those. But my reflection walks away without signing up for anything.

It moves on down the school hallway, students lined up in pairs or small groups along the lockers, my reflection cutting through the middle. When she waves to the others, they wave and smile in return. I can't help but smile to myself. I know I'm not hated at school. Like I told Sue B, people like me. But when my reflection passes each group of kids, they turn away and whisper to one another. Are they whispering about me? Something I did or said? The way I look? My smile disappears.

"Ask them what they're saying," I demand of my reflection.

The mirror-me whirls around in the hallway, watching my classmates sharing their secrets.

"Don't just stand there. Do something! You'd never let them talk about Sue B this way."

All at once, the students wave goodbye to the girl that is me in the shadows of the glass.

I don't understand. Where are they going? Why are they friendly yet secretive? I want to be a part of them, laughing and whispering on their way out of school. Instead, I'm left behind. Not one group of classmates asks me to join or pulls me along with them.

My hand extends toward the black surface, asking for my reflection's hand. Since when have we needed to be invited? We can go after them and find out what they're doing, make them include us.

The reflection does not reach back for me. It…she…heads farther down the wall once more. For the first time, I hesitate to follow. I'm getting too far away from Barnaby and Sue B. I should turn back. I'm about to retreat when it slams against the glass to get my attention. It hits the wall so hard that tiny cracks appear on the surface. Afraid of what will happen if I ignore it, I continue on, though I no longer feel the same as the girl inside.

The mirror image of me stands in my bedroom. Sue B is in the doorway, suitcases and bags piled around her, waving goodbye. This must be the moment Sue B leaves for college. Dad is behind her, reaching for the bags at her feet, ready to take her to the airport, and my reflection is frozen in place.

When my sister leaves the vision, I expect it to fade away and become some other moment of my life, real or imagined, but it doesn't change. Instead, we both look around the bedroom. I get closer to the wall as it points things out to me. On my walls are posters of movies I've seen with Sue B, bands she exposed me to. My desk has silly treasures from her, like cheap prizes from the Leaderboard and Christmas gifts throughout the years. I see a little stuffed pterosaur—a ridder—from my fifth birthday after we came back from the Ridderlands the second time. These memories and objects are mine, but they are Sue B's too. Then something occurs to me. There is nothing around me that is only mine. Everything has a trace of my sister. Everything that is me is also hers, and she was right. I don't know who I am without her.

Chapter Eighteen

The me that's in the mirror nods in our shared understanding and walks away, this time not down the length of the wall but into the depths of the black, shimmering glass.

I am alone and confused and missing my sister more now than ever. As if I still control a small bit of magic, I hear her voice.

"We have to find her."

"You almost drowned, Sue B. You need to rest."

That's not just wishful thinking. It's really her.

"Sue B," I yell out as I take off in her direction. Water splashes everywhere as I race along the shallow shoreline that washes up against the wall. It isn't long before I slam into my sister at full speed, knocking us both into the lapping waters.

"Careful," Barnaby scolds. "Let's try to keep her out of the water for a while."

But I don't release my squeeze around her waist, and she makes no move to stand or pull herself away.

"You're shaking. What happened?" she asks into the top of my head.

I don't know how to explain that without her, I'm only half a person, that I've always depended on her to define who I am. She knows this already. She tried to tell me, but Sue B can't understand how scary it is to know almost nothing about yourself. And the one thing that's holding this whole-messy-me together is flying across the country in a few months.

"You can't leave me." It's the only thing I feel certain about right now.

"You're the one that ran away from us," Sue B reminds.

"Not now, not ever."

Sue B releases her hug and grabs me by the shoulders so she can look me in the face. "Are you going to tell me what happened? Why you're acting this way?" I don't answer. "You're not four anymore, Jessie. You're old enough to talk through this without shutting down."

Barnaby reaches down and pulls us both up. "May I suggest we take this to dry land?"

We follow him in silence until we're beyond the black wall. It isn't enough time to sort my thoughts or think of what to say. I'm not used to this feeling of uncertainty. Usually, I'm confident, bold, and sure of myself. My self. What does that even mean? I'm not an independent being. More like a parasite feeding off my sister—a tick. Didn't she always used to call me a pest? Now she's finally got a chance to get rid of me, and all I can do is cling desperately on, burrowing deeper under her skin.

Okay, barf. I'm grossing myself out with my own comparison. But what happens to the tick when the dog gets its medicine? Do I shrivel up and die without her? Do I find someone else to base my whole personality off of? Will I ever get to be more than a pest?

"Talk to me," Sue B says, slumping to the ground, the exhaustion clear on her face.

"I don't know who I am."

"Is this about what I said? I meant that you need your own friends, your own hobbies, not that you don't have your own personality. You know who you are. You've been a ball of fire since the day you were born."

"The biggest, most important thing I've always been is your sister," I say.

"You'll always be my sister, but it's about time you become something more. You're too bright a star to be someone's something forever."

"You don't understand what it's like to have your life defined by someone else for so long and then suddenly have to make your own choices."

"Actually, she does," Barnaby interrupts. "I made it so your sister only had time to worry about me. I kept her from making friends. Sure, she was happy when it all stopped, but it can't have been easy to put herself out there after all I put her through. She did it, though. Made friends, got involved, found space to be who she should have always been if it weren't for me. She even found the courage to trust me again, and I messed it all up."

"Well, he didn't have it easy either. You know firsthand how hard it was for him to make new friends, to convince people he'd changed. You were there for what Ritter did to him. No one even remembers Barnaby the Bully anymore. He's become a really great person." Sue B's cheeks redden as she avoids looking at him. "The point is, everyone your age struggles with this stuff. Sure, some kids might have a head start, but middle school changes everything, and high school will change it all over again. No one really stays the same forever. You're going to figure it out."

"And what if no one wants to put up with me like you do?" I ask my sister.

"Then they're all stupid, because you're amazing."

Chapter Nineteen

I half expect the ground to shake. Sue B supporting me and making me feel valid, Barnaby admitting he messed up, and my sister sort of forgiving him—or at least admitting she still thinks he's great. If this were any other trip to the Ridderlands, we'd be on the path home.

But it's not. We're here because I thought this would solve everything. Instead, it's making it more complicated. So there's no quake. Just three people sitting wet on the side of a river with things half-said between them.

Barnaby stands and brushes off his damp jeans, though the sand clings stubbornly. "We can't stay here out in the open on the wrong side of the bank. We're lucky whoever is launching those boulders hasn't noticed us yet, but I don't want to push our luck."

Sue B and I follow his advice and stand, though no one seems sure of where to go from here.

"Anyone got any ideas?" I ask.

"Other than walking boldly into uncertain danger, any guesses how we get home?" Sue B is as lost as I am.

We both look to Barnaby for the answer, but he's locked in on something over my left shoulder. "Earth to Barnaby? Come in, Barnaby?"

"Do either of you see that?" he asks.

"See what?" we say together.

"There. Where the obsidian meets the sand."

"What the heck is obsidian?" I ask.

"All that black rock is called obsidian. Duh, Jessie." He is way too happy with himself.

"I don't think I like you anymore," I reply, narrowing my eyes at him.

"When molten lava hardens quickly, it forms that hard, glass-like rock," Sue B explains.

"Thank you, my favorite person in the Ridderlands." I smile at my sister, then return my glare to Barnaby.

"Okay, okay. Jokes aside, there's something sticking out of the ground there."

"Go see what it is," I nudge verbally while also pushing him physically. He resists my shove like a brick wall.

"Seriously," Sue B exclaims, "bunch of babies. I'll go."

She marches over to the spot like she's leading a full band and color guard. We watch cautiously, like she's approaching a mine instead, especially when she gets down on her hands and knees and starts digging around the object. When she doesn't explode, we approach her.

"What is it?" I ask.

"Some kind of tuber."

"Do you both pride yourselves on being walking encyclopedias? Define tuber, please."

"Maybe if you paid more attention in science class, you'd know these words too."

I roll my eyes at her. "For your information, earth science isn't until like eighth grade, and I have no idea when I'm supposed to learn what the heck a tuber is."

"Foods like potatoes and yams are tubers, Jessie. Your sister forgets we didn't all take advanced classes."

"You can't get back on my good side that easily, Mr. Obsidian." I punch him in the arm for good measure. "So...can we eat it then?

Because I'm super hungry."

"That's what I'm trying to figure out, if someone wants to help me dig it up."

Barnaby doesn't need to be asked twice. He's still trying to win my sister's forgiveness.

"Too bad Bruno's not here," I say. "He'd have it all dug up in minutes." I've missed that dog, I realize. "How's he doing, anyway?"

Without stopping his digging, Barnaby glances at me from time to time as he answers. "He's a lot older than the last time you saw him. Sleeps most of the day. Still such a good boy." He pulls a handful of what looks like fat roots from the ground. "Here we go. What do we think they are?"

Sue B takes one from his hand and inspects it. "I'm not sure, but it's nothing I recognize as poisonous, and no bright leaves to warn us off. I think I'm hungry enough to give it a try if we can figure out how to cook them."

"If we treat it like a potato, we'll need some kind of container and a fire to boil the water. We also haven't solved the problem of safety from exploding rocks. I feel like that's something of a priority."

"You're really caught up on this whole not dying by rock thing," I tease.

"Yeah, well, I'd really like us to make it to prom."

I'm not sure if Sue B notices the word "us" or the quick look her way, but I certainly do. Before I have a chance to catch her reaction, she's jumping to her feet. "I think I have an idea for the bowl."

She rushes over to a heavy stone about the size of her head and lifts it with a grunt. Then she lugs it over to another stone and drops it with a smash. The top rock cracks in half, and she reaches down to examine the remnants before holding one triumphantly over her head.

"Want to explain to the rest of the class what you're celebrating?" I ask.

"Isn't it obvious?" She's fully serious when she says this. "It's a geode."

"Again," I start, "there is nothing obvious about your earth science nerdery."

"Whatever, it's a geode, and there's a big enough hollow in the center to act as a bowl. I might have an answer to our heat source too. The obsidian, the geode, the volcanic soil our tubers are growing in, all these are signs of volcanic activity. We should be able to find a geyser or hot spring somewhere nearby to boil or steam our food." Sue B looks up at Barnaby, who is staring dumbly at her. "What? Don't tell me you don't get this either."

"You—you're amazing. Brilliant and amazing."

She grabs the tubers, her geode bowl—now filled with water—and races away with a heavy blush painted across her face.

Chapter Twenty

"Smooth," I whisper to Barnaby. I'm about to chase after my sister, leaving him to think over his next steps, when I realize I'm still barefoot. "You two didn't happen to grab my shoes before you swam over, did you? Not that I can call what Sue B was doing swimming."

"Watch it, Jessie. She risked her life to come after you."

"I know, and it was super scary, but I trusted that you wouldn't let anything happen to her. Especially with you being in love with her and everything."

"Is it that obvious?" he asks, covering his face with both hands.

"Apparently not to Sue B. I think she'll figure it out, though. You guys are gonna be fine. Now, any comment on my shoes?"

Barnaby pulls them from the pouch of his hooded sweatshirt and hands them over. They're a little damp from being in the pocket but not soaked. He must have chucked them across before diving in.

"Thanks," I say, slipping them onto my feet. "We should probably go find my sister before she gets too far."

Barnaby chuckles. "You're right. She's too caught up in science to remember us."

"Don't forget she's also running away from you." I stick out my tongue as I race past him.

It takes several minutes to track my sister down because she's gone farther than we anticipated. Luckily, the dripping from her wet clothes leaves a trail of plops in the dirt that take us right to her. Neither of us dares to speak as we approach her, though. She looks like a mad scientist, hunching over a hole in the ground with the geode bowl placed on top. The tubers are piled beside her feet except one, which she is currently hacking at with her house key.

"Have your keys on you?" Sue B asks Barnaby.

"Sure."

She tosses him a tuber. "Great, get peeling. Once we've removed the skin, we can cut the tuber into small pieces to make the cooking process faster."

"So that's what you're doing," I say suspiciously. "Definitely not taking out your feelings on an innocent tuber."

"Very funny, Jessie. You can take over with my keys." Sue B hands me the mutilated potatoish thing and goes back to watching the water.

"I'm a little confused by your plan," Barnaby admits. "I didn't think you could boil water using steam because it's already at boiling point."

"Ordinarily, you'd be right, but put your hand down on the ground."

Barnaby pulls his hand away quickly. "Wow, that's pretty hot."

"I believe this steam is superheated, meaning there's likely hot magma beneath the surface heating the steam well above the normal boiling point. If I'm right, we should be able to get our water temp high enough to cook with."

"You're saying there's lava under the Ridderlands now? What's going on in this place?"

"Volcanoes don't just appear. We have to assume it was always here, maybe dormant all those years before. And there *were* signs. Remember the geysers from the first time we came, when Barnaby guided us through the pattern." Sue B pauses briefly to laugh to herself. "We found them because you needed somewhere to go to the bathroom, and you insisted I sing your old potty song. I hated that song, but you loved it so much. For a whole year, you refused to go without it."

"That's so embarrassing! Stop talking now," I shriek.

"Hey, kiddo, I was there when it happened. No one here to be embarrassed for."

"Okay. Change the subject. Back to your boring earth science, please," I beg.

They both laugh at me but ease off. Though Sue B makes sure to roll her eyes as dramatically as possible. "You got my tuber ready?" she asks me.

I hold out the little hunks for her to see. "Small enough?"

"Perfect. Go ahead and toss them in. What about you, Barnaby?"

He holds up a tuber that looks like it's been gnawed on by a rabid raccoon. My sister and I both pull our faces wide. "What did you do to the poor thing?" I joke.

Sue B takes it and his keys away from him like she's afraid he might cause more damage. "Why don't you watch the water, and I'll handle the peeling."

After another half hour, Sue B deems the tubers soft enough to eat, and we all stare at each other to see who will be first to take a bite. I'm hungry, but I'm not starving enough to find the white, mushy lumps appetizing quite yet.

"I'd do it if there was butter and salt and pepper," I offer unhelpfully.

"It shouldn't be bad," Sue B says as if that's a winning recommendation, "just bland. I looked for sources of salt in the different rock types, but with only fresh water around, I didn't have any luck."

"Fine," Barnaby concedes, "I'll do it. But I want this to be remembered in the future."

He picks up the chunk of maybe-potato and closes his eyes as he places it on his tongue. Sue B and I watch intently as he mushes it around in his mouth before swallowing.

"Well?" I say.

Barnaby shrugs his left shoulder. "It's edible." Then he continues on to his next hunk.

"Before I do this, are you sure there isn't anything in your bag to make this better, maybe a ketchup packet from Speedy Burger?" I ask.

"You know I've already looked," Sue B says. "There's a stick of gum with some lint on the edges and a container of TicTacs. We can have some for dessert."

"I had one of Bruno's dog treats in my pocket, but it turned to a paste in the river, and I don't think any of us are that desperate."

"Yeah, I'll pass."

"We better get out of here quickly then. I don't know how long we can survive on tuber mush alone."

"Actually—"

I cut Sue B off. "This is one time I don't want to hear the science."

She holds up her hands in mock surrender.

Chapter Twenty-One

"I 've never enjoyed a TicTac more in my life," I proclaim. "Even if they are a little water-damaged."

"I guess we can cancel your application to Survivor," Sue B jokes.

Our laughter is interrupted by the geode bowl, still resting on top of the volcanic vent, suddenly launching into the air with a burst of superheated vapor.

"Run!" Sue B screams, grabbing me by my arm and practically pulling it out of its socket to get away from the blast area.

Though we're running as hard and fast as we can, tiny droplets of burning water hit our exposed skin with a sizzle, and I start screaming. Barnaby rushes to my side and pulls me and Sue B beneath him like a shield, taking all of the scalding water across his back. He doesn't groan or scream, only winces as each burn lands.

Below us, the ground tremors. But this is no ordinary earthquake. The earth begins to ripple like a wave rolling to the shore.

"What's happening?"

"I should have seen the signs," Sue B shouts over the noise. "We have to get farther away. Now!"

Barnaby doesn't wait for further explanation. He lifts us both in the air—one in each arm—and carries us toward the river. "We need to get back across."

I waste no time before diving in. It's only once I reach the shore that

I remember my sister can't swim well.

Sue B stands frozen in place as Barnaby tries to shake the fear from her. "I'm going to get you across," he says. "Do you hear me?"

Her head shakes in tiny, sharp nods.

"I'm gonna throw you as far as I can so you won't need to swim far. I'll be right behind you, and your sister is right in front of you. We will not let you drown."

Sue B's nods turn to resistance and her eyes widen at his words. "Don't, don't."

He ignores her protests and lifts her like she weighs nothing. "Ready?"

Neither of us is ready for this, but we have no choice.

Barnaby launches her like a dad might do on a hot summer day in the backyard pool. As soon as she hits the water, I start swimming back toward her, totally unsure of my ability to save her and hoping Barnaby will make quick work of getting there.

My sister surges above the water when I'm only a few feet from her position. The memory of her nearly pulling Barnaby under earlier fills my mind. If I'm going to be any help to her, I need her to calm down.

"Don't thrash!" I yell out. "Remember the quicksand and lie back. Let the water keep you afloat."

To my surprise, she listens.

"Chin up! Chin up!" I yell as her head dips below the water's surface. I get to her side and tip her head into the right position, using my arm under her neck to make her feel safe.

Barnaby is there a second later, helping to keep her buoyed and guiding us toward the safety of the far shore. Exhausted, we climb out and collapse into the sand and grass. Sue B in the middle grabs both of our hands in hers and pulls them over her heart.

"I can't…believe…you threw…me!" Her chest heaves up and down as she tries to catch her breath.

"There wasn't any time to convince you. I just acted. No way was I going to lose you to this horrible place."

But this horrible place has other plans. Even on this side of the river, we aren't completely safe. On top of the swelling ground and spewing geysers, I sit up to see smoke rising into the sky in the distance and a fast-moving boulder headed our way.

"Move!" I yell, rolling to my side and forgetting my injured knee in my haste to get up. "Incoming!"

Everyone is scrambling with no sense of where we're going. I'm not sure Barnaby and Sue B even know what they are running from. The thing about a place like this is that we believe it when someone says "go" and worry about questions later. Better to be a fool than a dead fool. As the only one with all the information, I need to take charge.

"To the trees," I order.

We're finally moving in one direction when the boulder explodes overhead. It might just be pebbles that hail down on us from above because of whatever force field is at work, but they still sting and leave little red welts behind, adding to our new burn marks.

Back where we started, under the relative safety of the canopy, we assess our wounds and watch as plumes of fire, rock, and ash are released into the sky across the river.

Chapter Twenty-Two

"Is that the volcano?" I ask.

"These are just warning signs," Sue B answers. "But an eruption is coming, that's for sure. And it's going to be a heck of a lot worse."

Barnaby groans, then kicks the trunk of the tree. "I don't understand what this world wants from us. There's no way we're going back over the river into an active volcanic site. Are we just here to watch as it's all destroyed? Is that what you want?" he screams into the sky. "Well, no thanks. I've had enough of the Ridderlands for a lifetime, and I don't care what happens to it. Burn the whole thing to ashes, and let us go home." He crumbles to the ground with no more fight left in him.

"Feel better?" I say. He doesn't even raise his head in annoyance.

Maybe I should tell him the real reason we're stuck here. That I'm a complete idiot who thought that without Ritter this place would turn into a paradise where all our problems faded away. He'll be angry and probably never speak to me again, but at least he won't be picking fights with the trees anymore.

I can't, though. It would really suck to lose Barnaby, like, really suck, but spending the last few months with my sister refusing to talk to me would be unbearable. No, I'll find another way to deal with the guilt. If I can't give them the truth, I can still give them a reason. Something to focus on and hopefully buy me time to figure out a way home.

"I think I know why we're here," I declare, then wait for them to take the bait.

Sue B moves closer first but says nothing. It's only when Barnaby shifts so he's facing me that I continue.

"Every time we've been here, there's been some kind of conflict or lie or whatever. And every time we find the answers, you two get closer, right? Enemies to understanding one another, then friends, and now…"

They both look anywhere except at each other.

"Fine, you two can avoid the obvious forever and start thinking of the Ridderlands as home, or you can finally admit what you're both too chicken to say. I'm obviously here to face the fact that Sue B is leaving and I need to become my own person or whatever, so I'll be home missing you guys while no one else in the world remembers you exist." For an added nudge in the right direction, I add, "Not even Hillary Tanzen." That should get them talking—or at least arguing. "I'm going to give you two some space while I contemplate my pathetic existence."

"Wait," Sue B says. "You can't drop that all on us and then walk away without an explanation. Did you have a dream? Does this have something to do with the obsidian? We've had no clear indicators from this place about what's going on, and now with volcanoes threatening to erupt, you have all the answers? I'm used to you thinking you're right about everything, but something's not right about your sudden realization." She crosses her arms, tightens her lips, and raises her left eyebrow.

"I'm just putting all the pieces of the puzzle together."

"And when did you have time to put that all together? When we were being burned with scalding hot water vapor, swimming for our lives across a river, or being pelted with shards of rock?" she asks.

"Be honest, Jessie." Barnaby reaches over and places a hand on my shoulder.

Uh, I can't be honest, Barnaby. The two of you will kill me!

There's only one thing I can do: hit 'em with the half-truth. "All right. You caught me. I hate that you two haven't worked out this prom thing. You both mean so much to me, and you've been a complete mess, Sue B. I know you told me not to meddle in your business and to let you handle the situation, but you can't blame me for trying."

"Jess, I know you feel like you always have to fix everything, but Barnaby and I are practically adults. We'll figure it out eventually." For the first time in a while, they truly look at one another. "We've got more important problems than prom dates to solve."

I really didn't think this plan through. First, I made the mistake of thinking it would be safe to take a timeout from the real world. Then, we're abandoned by the ridders who I thought were my magic friends. Now, it's too chaotic with the world literally ready to burn down to accomplish the one thing this whole trip was meant to accomplish.

"You look like your younger self when you pout like that," Sue B points out.

"I'm not pouting," I say, unamused, but before I know it, the two of them have dog-piled on me with a hug.

Chapter Twenty-Three

A vibration like a cat's purr trembles beneath us, then it aggressively builds. The whole pile of us lifts into the air and crashes back down, like someone is flicking the gravity switch off and on. And it keeps happening. The effect becomes stronger and stronger with each passing impact. A thunderous uproar draws closer every time, a storm approaching from a distance that I know will wreak havoc when it arrives.

Sue B and Barnaby are taking the brunt of the injury as they cradle me between their bodies. I'm grateful, but I know this must be taking a toll, especially after our other wounds from the last hour. "What"—BAM!—"should we do?"

"Hold on"—SLAM!—"until it"—CRASH!—"stops!" Right as Barnaby finishes his sentence, everything ceases and the word "stops" rings out like a bell.

I weakly crawl away from our clump, wincing as the ground bites into the gash on my knee, but too afraid I'll fall down if I try to stand. Sue B is the first to right herself, though she sticks her arms out to balance and half squats.

"Need help up?" she asks Barnaby.

"I think I'll stay here for a while."

"Umm…guys!" I scramble up using the side of a tree trunk to steady myself. "You have to see this."

Lined up along the far shore of the river is something I can only imagine seeing in a nightmare. Giants made of stone, enough to form an army. They are all different colors: pinks, grays, sandstone, and some even with gold streaks. I bet Sue B could name every rock, but what could I call these monsters that would do justice to the level of fear that they are filling me with?

"Rock golems," Barnaby says in awe.

"I'm sorry, rock what?" Sue B asks.

"A golem is a type of elemental. A creature made up of some kind of inanimate material. In this case, rocks."

"And you know this how?"

"I play a lot of fantasy games, RPGs, stuff like that. The thing is, they are usually created using magic, and their creator holds power over them to make them do whatever he or she wants. This isn't just nature, like the volcanoes; this is intentional, and I can only think of one person who would have the power to create something like this. One person who really hates us and wants to see us destroyed more than anything."

"But Ritter is dead," I argue. "We watched the ridders tear him apart."

"We watched until they flew away with him. None of us actually saw him die."

"If you're right," says Sue B, "that explains why the ridders took off. But how did he convince them to bring us here in the first place? They must hate him as much as we do. Look what he's done to their home."

My stomach sinks. It could be so much worse for me if they figure out what I did on their own.

"Maybe he's got something he's holding over them?" Barnaby guesses. "Some threat or truce they came to."

"How did he get away from them in the first place?" I ask, trying to bring the conversation back to focusing on Ritter.

"Anything we came up with would only be a guess at this point. However he did it, he's the only explanation for what's happening that makes any sense."

Barnaby's right. And thankfully, his statement is enough to stop questioning the motives of the ridders. "What do you think the golems want?" I ask. "Or Ritter, rather."

"To finish what he started, once and for all."

I'm usually pretty tough. Not one to break down in fear, but I can't help the tears that flow from my eyes when Barnaby says that. Ritter wants us dead—and I led us right into his path.

Chapter Twenty-Four

Sue B and Barnaby don't know that Ritter had no way of knowing we were coming. We might be tangled up in this mess now, but it wasn't meant for us. I have to assume this is a punishment for the ridders based on everything I know. If Ritter really survived, it makes sense he'd turn on them for helping us and attacking him. I knew there had to be a reason they left their nests behind. They also warned me it's only safe away from rocks. This could be why they didn't answer me at first when I called them to me. But I begged. I wouldn't give up, and I left them no choice but to bring us back here. Now we're stuck.

If I tell my sister and Barnaby the truth, we can go after the ridders and beg them to bring us home. If I continue to hide my secret betrayal, they'll keep on assuming Ritter is attacking us personally and think we need to win the battle in order to get out of here. Especially if they assume the ridders are collaborating with Ritter.

"Oh no!" I heave over with my hands on my stomach as guilt rises up my throat. A little deep breathing does nothing to solve the light-headedness or nausea.

"What's wrong?" Sue B asks, a flash of panic in her eyes. "Was the tuber poison?"

I don't think I can do this. They can't know this is all my fault. I hunch down and rock back and forth on my heels. Fingertips catching me from falling flat on my face. We could all die if I don't say something, but my life is over if I do.

"Barnaby," my sister calls, "help me with her."

That's when the sky lights up so brightly that for a moment I think the sun is rising to reveal my home world. But if the sun is rising, it's also falling from the sky and crashing into the ground. We're plummeted into the purple darkness once more.

"What new hell is this?" Barnaby asks.

The sickness disappears as I stand in awe of what we're seeing.

"It could be volcanic rock crumbling from the lava and forced out from the pressure, or a mixture of the lava and these golems throwing their boulders. I…I…It's hard to know. Does anyone see a smoke or ash plume? I can't even tell where the volcano's summit is." Sue B's earth science is failing her as magic and mayhem collide before our eyes.

It's hard to look away. An army of rock golems framing a background of flaming boulders cutting through the sky, beautiful and horrifying at the same time. But we're not safe. "We can't stay here. The river's protective magic might not be enough to stop everything Ritter is planning to attack with." I have to try to save them, even if I'm too much of a coward to tell the truth just yet.

"Where can we go?" my sister asks.

"We should find the ridders. Maybe I can convince them to get us out of here. It's better than the alternative."

"I don't see any other option, Sue B. I think this is one of those times we have to trust Jessie." Barnaby smiles at me. A smile I definitely don't deserve, just like his trust. "If there was some way to fight, you know I would, but we can't win against all of that."

"You're both right. I can feel the temperature heating up already. Let's just hope the ridders are still on our side and don't hand us right over to Ritter once we find them."

We're beat up, hungry, and thirsty. My knee is throbbing, but I don't dare complain since everything is my fault. Periodically, we stop and I try to summon the ridders, though I know even if there is magic in this world, I no longer deserve it.

"How are you holding up, Jess?" Sue B asks.

Despite my insistence that the sick feeling has passed, she keeps stopping every half hour or so to check in with me. I roll my eyes and keep walking, not because she deserves my attitude, but because I'll break down if I try to talk right now.

Though I'm walking ahead of them, I hear Barnaby approach her and whisper, "She's tough. She'll be fine."

I hope we'll all be fine.

"How much farther do we walk before we give up on finding them?" Sue B whispers back.

I can't blame them for questioning my plan when we've been out here in mostly open fields for nearly two hours with no sign of our flying friends—if they are our friends. There's no other way to get home, though. No dreams to guide us or gentle quakes to validate our actions. If I ask for a rest, I can buy some time to convince them both to keep going.

"I changed my mind. I have to stop." The grove of trees off to the right is a perfect place to hunker down and think, so I go straight there.

"Guess we're taking a break under those trees." Barnaby is the first to follow after me.

Before either of them can reach me, I see a spot of red among the green leaves above me. My body is exhausted, but I start climbing branch by branch until I reach it.

"What are you doing now?" Sue B rushes over and reaches up after me. "Get down here before you break something. The last thing we need is a broken leg."

"How about an apple?" I say as I toss one down. "Or three."

Finally, something is breaking my way. Sweet apple juice trickles down my throat, quenching my thirst while satisfying my hunger. Sue B insists on climbing up when we all want more. We eat until we've each had our fill.

"Now I need a nap," Barnaby says, lying back into the grass.

"Do you think that's safe?" asks Sue B.

"We can't even see the golems or the river anymore. What's to be scared of out here?"

"I know you want the riders to solve all our problems, Jessie, but we still don't know if they're working with Ritter again."

"Look around you, sis. Even if Ritter found some way to threaten the riders, that doesn't explain the contrast between the two sides of the river, like the magical field that blocks the lava and rocks from crossing over. We haven't been attacked once since we've started looking for them. Heck, we just ate real food that their trees provided for us," I remind them.

"You're right. I'm...I'm just scared," Sue B admits.

"We're all scared. But I think your sister is trying to say we're safe right now. And we could all use a rest."

Chapter Twenty-Five

S leep comes quickly now that our stomachs are full. At first, I'm drifting and waking from the aches and pains, but after a couple of nodding blinks, I'm out like a light.

There are flames everywhere in my dream. Fireballs flare through the purple sky, and lava flows surround me as I stand on an island of grass under the fruit tree I know I'm really sleeping under. Sue B and Barnaby are gone, leaving me all alone.

"My, my, how you've grown, little Jessie Jess," a voice echoes over the chaos.

Every muscle squeezes into a ball at the sound. Though I've never heard his voice myself, I know exactly who's talking. It's Ritter. It has to be.

"What do *you* want?" I ask like I'm spitting out a rotten taste.

"That's no way to speak to an old friend, now is it?"

"Ha. More like a mortal enemy."

"Think what you want, but I only ever tried to help your sister rid herself of her biggest problem. It's not my fault she didn't have the guts to see it through." His voice softens as he tries to convince me.

"You're the only problem she needs to get rid of. How are you back after the ridders attacked you?" If I have to talk to this jerk, at least I can get some information from him.

He laughs in response to me. "I'm not so quickly disposed of. I created the ridders, and I can destroy them just as easily. Did you really think my own creation could be my undoing?"

Ritter must have used his magic to escape the last time we were here. Now he's creating a whole new army to destroy the ridders for their betrayal.

"If they're so easy to destroy, how come it's taken you all these years to get around to it?" Maybe it's not smart to challenge him like this, but even if it feels like a nightmare, it's still my dream, and I'm not going to let him push me around.

"It takes time to amass an army of this scale. Why have you come here? To interfere?" he asks.

I freeze, hoping he can't read my mind, sense my guilt. As he's only a looming voice, I don't know what he can see. "Don't worry about us, we'll be out of here as soon as we can be."

"You think the ridders will save you again? It was my choice to let them bring you in without attacking, and I won't be so magnanimous again."

"Being bitter that we always get away from you is no reason to make up words."

"Being responsible for dragging your sister and her oversized oaf here against their will doesn't mean I need to give you a pass, either."

He knows! But how?

"Shut up. You don't know anything about why we're here," I protest.

"On the contrary, I know you used your last bit of magic to beg for a return ride. The ridders aren't the only ones that heard your calls. But perhaps your sister would like to know what you've done."

"Don't—"

"Maybe I already have." His voice fades away with his last words, leaving me alone in this nightmare of fire.

I'm soaked in sweat when I wake up. Sue B is hovering over me with her face crinkled in concern.

"Thank God, you're finally awake," she says, pulling me into a hug.

"What do you mean, *finally*?"

"Are you kidding me? You've been asleep for two hours, and I've been shaking you and calling your name."

"And you've got a fever," Barnaby adds.

"It's not a fever, it's from the fire," I say.

"Fire? What fire?"

"Ritter called to me. There was fire and lava everywhere. He's trying to destroy the ridders, and that's not all."

"Jessie, you said yourself you have no magic. And neither of us had dreams. Don't you think it's possible this was the fever and not a message from Ritter? Your knee is probably infected." Sue B is seriously worried, and she's got me wondering if I made the whole thing up. "We should have taken the time to clean your wound when we were near the river. There's no way we can make it back there now."

Sue B helps me sit up and I pull my knee toward me. "It doesn't look any worse than it did before. No purple, no pus…" I give my knee a sniff. "And it doesn't smell funky."

"Can I?" Barnaby reaches forward to touch my leg, and I nod my permission. "It really doesn't feel that swollen, Sue B."

"What about the fever, though?" she asks.

"The dreams we've had before were trying to help us, brought on by Jessie's magic, right? It's not completely impossible to believe that Ritter's magic can bring on fiery nightmares and seep into this world. I think we should keep an eye on the knee and monitor Jessie for fever, but either way, we need to find the ridders and get out of here."

"There's just one small problem with that," I say to Barnaby. "In my dream, Ritter said a lot of words I didn't understand, but the gist of it is that he isn't going to let us back through. Something about being magmous, like blocking us with the lava?"

"Magnanimous," Sue B corrects. "He's basically saying he isn't going to be generous or do us any favors. In other words, we're stuck here."

Chapter Twenty-Six

"There has to be a way out," Barnaby protests. "The world guided us home before even though he was trying to trap us, why can't that happen again?"

"I don't know what's changed in the last five years, but between the rock monsters and the lava formations, it doesn't seem like the world is on our side anymore. Maybe it wasn't last time either. We had to work out a deal with the ridders to get home."

"Ritter mentioned my magic being gone. I think it was the magic helping us before, not the world itself. We're on our own unless we can convince the ridders to fight," I say.

"Why would they fight when they can hide?" Barnaby asks, hopelessness mixing with his words.

"Maybe they won't, but we have to try. It might be our only hope." I'm not willing to give up. This is my fault and my problem to fix. "If you guys don't want to come with me, I understand."

"Whoa, whoa, whoa. You're not going anywhere by yourself. Not with a possible fever and infected leg wound." Sue B crosses her arms.

"So you're coming with me?"

"You're not really leaving us much choice," jokes Barnaby. "Lead the way."

Every so often, I close my eyes and reach my mind toward the ridders. I might not have magic anymore, but that doesn't mean they can't listen. They are creatures born with magic. Created from Ritter's dark powers and changed by their own choices. If the force field along the river remains strong despite their absence, then it makes sense their own magic is far-reaching. Enough to hear a young girl begging for help.

The farther we get from the river, the lusher the greenery around us becomes. Fruit fills nearly every tree we pass. Varieties that have no reason to grow so close together: apples, oranges, bananas—even coconuts. Little brooks and creeks trickle through the grasses. Nothing as big as the river we crossed, but enough to provide a cool drink and water to clean my wound.

"Your head is much cooler," Sue B remarks.

"I told you it wasn't a fever."

"Let's save the 'I told you so' until after we're safely home," Barnaby says, stepping between us. "We need all of our strength for the battle ahead."

He's totally right. Bickering with Sue B at home is totally different than arguing while a madman threatens to unleash a volcano to destroy everything. "Sorry, sis."

"It's fine. I'm more worried about whether we're heading in the right direction or not. The surroundings are improving, but there's still no sign of the ridders. You'd think we'd see nests or something."

I'm frustrated too. I didn't think it would take this long to track them down, but flying creatures can cover a lot more land than a couple of walking humans.

Rising from where I've been splashing in the creek, I stand to go on.

"Wait," Sue B whispers to me as she grabs my shoulder and whirls me around toward Barnaby. He's completely lost in thought, eyes narrowed and searching upward, chin in his hand. All at once, he snaps out of it.

"Maybe we've been going about this all wrong. We're trying to track down the ridders, who could be hundreds of miles away by now, maybe thousands, when we should be figuring out a way to bring them to us."

"I've been trying to call them, Barnaby. There's no answer—if my message is even getting through."

"I'm talking about doing something to get their attention. Something so big they won't be able to ignore it."

"Why are you grinning like that?" Sue B asks.

Barnaby responds by widening his smile further.

"This is going to be good," I say, giving him a high-five.

Chapter Twenty-Seven

Barnaby's plan is more than good, it's straight up brilliant. We're gathering stones, as large as we can carry, and stacking them in the creek. Once we have enough to form a wall twice as tall as the depth of the water level, Barnaby shoves bits of twigs and plant matter into any gaps, creating a working dam. From there, he climbs the nearest tree, then throws the fruit down. He picks every single orange on this tree before moving on. At the top of the tree, he uses the strength of his legs to snap branches under his weight. The tree looks like it's been hit by a major tornado by the time he's finished with it. He even has me and Sue B stomp the oranges into the ground. Wasting food while we fight for survival is a bizarre feeling, but we need to draw attention to ourselves.

The teens won't let me climb because of my knee, even though I try to convince them that stomping fruit is worse for my injury. All that gets me is banned from both jobs and left to strip leaves from low-hanging branches. With an open invitation to create destruction, there has to be something more that I can do.

Fire would be the best way to draw the ridders' attention. After all, we want them to think that the enemy has crossed into their territory and fire is the enemy's weapon. But we don't have any matches or lighters, and the lava is miles behind us. There are no mirrors or magnifying glasses. Barnaby says even if we had a fire starter, all of the wood here is too green and full of life to burn easily.

Sue B climbs down from a nearby tree and comes to my side. "What do you think? Is it enough to piss off the ridders?"

Four trees are badly broken but not in a way that won't grow back, branches and twigs are thrown across an area no bigger than our living room, and fruit of every kind is smashed beyond rescue, though the seeds will grow new trees. Even the dam, which I thought of as our biggest attack, did little more than create a dripping pool around the rock wall.

"I'm not sure it's a Ritter-level wreck."

"You're right. It reminds me more of a Jessie Jess invasion of my bedroom from years ago," she says with a smirk.

I don't know if that's a jab or a gentle joke, so I shrug it off.

If the ridders wanted to stop our destruction, they'd be here already. What we're doing either isn't enough, or the message isn't getting through, like trying to send a text, but the cell tower is down. This whole plan is based on the idea that the ridders' magic created the trees and fruit and creeks, but how exactly is the magic connecting the trees to our flying friends?

My mind races with ways things are connected: satellites, radio towers, power lines, power cords, cables, and...

"Hey, Barnaby," I call out. He hops down from the tree he's currently demolishing. "Think you could pull a tree completely out of the ground if we found one small enough? I'm wondering if the magical connection is through the roots."

"I could try." He shrugs. "It would be a lot easier if Bruno were here to dig the roots up first."

A cluster of saplings grows across the creek. I give a tug and find only the slightest resistance as I pull. The baby tree must not have developed a complex root system yet—according to my sister. If we want to send a message by "unplugging" a tree from the magic, we'll need something a little better connected.

"What about this one?" Sue B asks, tugging. "Too strong for me to pull out, but it does have a little give."

Barnaby braces himself in a squat with both hands, squeezing the narrow tree trunk as if he's trying to strangle it. On a count of three, he pulls with his arms and pushes upward with his leg muscles.

The tree shifts two inches out of the dirt before seeming to pull back, like a child refusing to come along.

He shakes it off and assumes a pulling position once more, this time waving Sue B over to help him. With the two of them pulling, the tree manages to lift even less.

"How is that possible?" I ask, hoping Sue B's earth science expertise will have an explanation.

"I think the tree is resisting—or the roots are pulling back? I'm not sure. It feels like we're playing tug-of-war."

"Then I'm right about the magic connecting through the root systems!" I celebrate my big-brain moment with a dance.

"Don't get ahead of yourself," Barnaby warns. "We still need to get this sucker out of the ground if we want to send a big enough message. I doubt two pathetic tugs are enough to draw them out of hiding."

I stop mid-floss to consider the problem.

"Maybe all three of us should try pulling?" Sue B asks.

"Yes, but we all need to pull different trees."

Barnaby's face contorts. "What are you talking about, Jessie?"

"Have neither of you won a game of tug-of-war? Winning is all about saving the big pulls for when your competition is least expecting them. You need to catch them off balance."

"So if we pull from different spots, the roots won't know when the real pull is coming?" Barnaby asks.

"You got it. Now spread out and find a tree."

Within a couple of minutes, the three of us stand ready to yank with all our might. Barnaby goes first, sticking with the same tree he's been working on. We want to lure the magic into a false sense of confidence, thinking Barnaby is going to keep trying with no success. While he's mid-pull, Sue B yanks on a slightly smaller tree, splitting the magic's attention. For a moment, Barnaby's tree yields as the magic shifts to protect Sue B's, but within a few seconds, both trees are pulled back toward the ground.

Everyone stops tugging. We wait, pretending to accept defeat. Then, on my call, we all pull at once. Somehow, the magic is ready for us. I yell for Sue B to scramble around yanking other trees at random. Barnaby rushes over to my sister's previous tree and gives a firm tug while the magic guesses where to fight back. Finally, everyone rushes over to my tree and yanks together, heaving the tree with all our might.

The roots rise from the ground, but still the magic won't let go. I drop down and shove my arms into the hole the tree is leaving behind, hoping I can keep them from slipping back into the dirt.

A shock of power shoots through my hands, up my arms, and into my chest. I fly backward from the jolt and Sue B and Barnaby release their hold and race after me.

Barnaby scans my body for injuries.

"Jessie, are you okay?" My sister's voice is frantic as she lifts my head onto her lap.

"I…I feel…powerful!"

Chapter Twenty-Eight

"Um, care to clarify?" Barnaby asks.

"Like full of magic. More than I ever had before," I answer.

"Are you sure you're not just in shock from being electrocuted, or whatever just happened to you?" Sue B suggests.

"Could electrocution do this?" I hold my hand out to Sue B and produce a bottle of her favorite juice without any effort. No squinting my eyes or shaking in concentration. The magic surges back and forth through my veins like I'm made of the stuff.

"Holy—"

"This is incredible. Think I could get a ham-and-cheese sandwich on rye with mustard? And a pickle." I hand the sandwich over to Barnaby, who licks his lips before taking the first bite. "Tastes just like my mom made it."

"I wasn't sure what kind of cheese you liked, so I asked for it just the way you like it."

"Food is great," Sue B says, "and I could definitely go for something besides fruit, but I really hope your magic can do more than feed us."

"Well, what do you want it to do?"

"Taking us home would be great."

It seems right to close my eyes for something this big. Images of home fill my mind as I ask for a way out. There's no shaking of the ground telling me it worked, so I open my eyes to see if anything has changed.

Sue B and Barnaby are staring at me with hope twinkling in their eyes, but besides a scattering of crumbs down the front of Barnaby's shirt in place of the sandwich I gave him, everything is the same.

"Doesn't look like leaving is going to be that easy," I say. "Sorry."

"What about the ridders? Can you sense where they are? Call to them? Send them a message for help?" Sue B's questions come out like a snowball rolling downhill and picking up speed.

I reach out to the creatures, casting a visual net over the Ridderlands, hoping to catch some trace of them. It's like they've disappeared completely. Would they really bring us here and abandon us to this war with Ritter? Desert their homes over this threat? I know I begged them to bring us here, but leaving us to die is way worse than ignoring my call in the first place. How can they think this is a favor repaid?

"It doesn't feel like they're out there anywhere."

"That's impossible. They can't just leave us here." Barnaby echoes my own disbelief.

"Do they expect us to fight this war all on our own?" Sue B asks.

I hate that they're both looking to me for answers. Only a few moments ago I felt powerful and full of joy to sense the magic within me once again, but it's nothing more than a burden when these two are staring at me like I'm their only hope.

"Listen," I start. "We've solved our own problems here a million times. Overcoming every obstacle this world has thrown at us—Ritter has thrown at us. Between the three of us, I know we can find a way out." I turn to my sister. "Sue B, what can we do to stop the lava?" Then I look at Barnaby. "Think about everything you know about the rock golems. Weaknesses and stuff. Anything we can use to defeat them. I've got this magic and your knowledge; there's no way I'm going to let a little thing like war stop me from getting home. With or without the ridders' help."

"Judging from the obsidian wall back across the river, that water has the ability to stop the lava in its tracks. In our world, water has failed as a diversion method, only slowing the results of the lava. It has to be a mixture of the river and the magic that makes up the force field. Though we don't know how the ridders did it before. If you could figure out how to manipulate both, you might have a chance to keep the lava from overtopping the river bed."

"So I need to do what? Create a force field like the one at the river and go all Avatar waterbender to hold the lava back and harden it?" I confirm with Sue B.

"Something like that. Maybe a deep ditch on the other side to slow the lava down even more. That's all the science I've got for this one. No one has ever had much success halting 2,000-plus degrees of molten magma in its tracks."

"I guess it's a good thing we've got magic on our side."

"Wouldn't it be more helpful if all of us had magic?" Barnaby asks.

"Sure, but something tells me it doesn't work that way. I'm the only one that has ever had it. You're welcome to grab some roots and see what happens, though."

Sue B and I position ourselves back at the tree ready to pull while Barnaby lies on his stomach. "One…two…three!" I shout. We yank as hard as we can. This time, the tree doesn't fight us like it did before. Barnaby plunges his hands down into the root hole and comes back up with a handful of dirt and nothing more.

He wipes his hands on his jeans. "Nothing. Not even a tingle." I open my mouth to reply, but he puts a finger to my lips. "If the word 'duh' comes out of your mouth, I'm going to lose it."

I laugh and throw my hands up in surrender. "Why don't you focus on a plan for the golems while Sue B and I practice with the water?"

The creek is a lot smaller than the river, but it's a good place to start.

"Try pushing the water through the dam. I want to see if you can increase the force of the flow."

First, I position myself on the side of the dam where the water is built up, assuming that pushing will be easier than pulling—based on absolutely no facts at all. I can feel the water wriggle beneath my magical grasp as I concentrate on it. It's almost like it wants to be controlled. My hands push out in front of me. If TV has taught me anything, this is the way to do it. The rocks of the dam shift very slightly before settling again. It's definitely not enough to stop a volcanic eruption, and I've already got a trickle of sweat rolling down my back from exertion.

"This is a lot harder than I thought it would be," I tell Sue B.

"Maybe don't try to force it so much. Think of it more like convincing the water to act than making it do what you want. Kind of like I have to do with you." Sue B sticks out her tongue.

"We've got a war to win, but I'm not going to forget you said that."

I focus back on the wriggly willingness of the water that I first felt. Then, I imagine the most powerful water I can. Raging floods uprooting houses and trees. Waterfalls plunging over cliffs with a thunderous roar. Rapids weaving in and out of rocky passes. The water gets excited beneath my grasp. Energy is building in every molecule until it shoves forward into the rock pile, knocking over the stones and flowing freely to the other side.

Chapter Twenty-Nine

"Think you can do that on a much larger scale?" Sue B asks. I nod confidently. "Then that's one problem down."

"What can you tell me about golems, Barnaby?"

Instead of a straight answer, I get a breakdown of facts that span several different video games. Apparently, they are elementals immune to fire and lava. In some games, they are susceptible to water and ice, but in others, they can only be defeated with blunt force attacks. He goes on for nearly fifteen minutes before I cut him off.

"Do you know anything for certain, or are these all just guesses?" I ask.

"It's not my fault you asked your sister about factual science and asked me about video game lore. I'm trying to be as specific as possible, but all of this is made up."

"Except the real-life rock golems we have to face across the river."

"Right." He shrugs at Sue B.

"Let's just assume the water doesn't hurt them because that seems like it would be too easy to knock out both of Ritter's attacks with one move. What kind of blunt force attacks are we talking about?"

"If we're playing Ark, then a Giganotosaurus could do it—or explosives," he adds. Like I'm carrying a backpack of TNT.

"I somehow don't think creating another magical dino creature is going to make anything simpler," I say.

"It could be pretty cool to unleash a Jurassic attack on his side of the force field." I can totally tell from Barnaby's eyes that he's imagining it as he suggests it.

"Let's save that for a plan B," Sue B interrupts.

"What about lightning?" I offer. "That's kind of like explosives."

"According to experiments with lightning and rocks, if they are made out of harder rock like granite, lightning strikes aren't strong enough to break the rocks."

"Dang it. There has to be some way to take them down."

"There's one option we haven't discussed yet," Barnaby says. "The golems are connected to Ritter by his magic. It's what allows him to control them. If we take out Ritter—"

"We take out the rock golems!" I finish his thought.

"I doubt Ritter is going to be out in plain sight waiting for us to knock him out, though." My sister is always so logical.

"But if my magic can sense his magic, then I might be able to locate him. That would give us a chance to end the war very quickly. We'll need to keep him busy fighting our water attacks for that to work."

"And since you're the only one with magic, that means one of us will have to sneak across and try to take out Ritter." Sue B's voice is quiet and wavering.

"I guess that means me," Barnaby says. "Sue B isn't going to get across the river without drowning on her own. Besides, after what he did to me, I'm ready to face him. He needs to be stopped once and for all."

"Are we really going to do this?" Sue B asks.

Barnaby puts his arm around her shoulders and she blushes. "I don't think we have any choice."

"We think we know how to destroy the golems, but we still need a way to slow them down while Barnaby goes after Ritter. He needs to be fully engaged in our attack if this plan stands a chance," I say.

"This would be so much easier if we had the ridders fighting with us," Sue B complains. "I guess we lead with the water attack and see if that has an impact on the golems. At least we know it'll put out the fireballs, and as long as the force field still stands, we won't get crushed by boulders. It's a starting place."

"So are we ready to head back toward the river?" I ask. Part of me is excited to take on the challenge, but another voice in my head is sending out a warning. *This isn't a dream. It's real life, and you could totally die here and take your sister and Barnaby with you.*

Barnaby takes a huge breath in, and his whole body shudders as he lets it out. "Let's do this."

Chapter Thirty

From the moment we turn back, it's clear something isn't right. The trees are losing leaves, and the grass is slightly yellow. There are bare patches where the grass has completely withered away and died. This all seems impossible. Weren't we just here a few hours ago?

Out of curiosity, we stop at a couple of trees we know for a fact were growing fruit the first time we passed through, but there isn't a single apple, orange, or pear to be found. Which, to be honest, is really freaking me out because I can only think of two explanations for what's going on:

1. The ridders really are leaving forever, and the magic of this side of the river is fading away with them.
2. When I absorbed the magic from the tree roots, I somehow managed to steal the magic from this side of the river.

If either of these is true, we might be screwed.

Our plan depends on a full river and active force field if we're to have any hope of winning—and staying alive. Since the river area is the farthest away, it makes sense it would be the worst off due to a lack of magic in scenario one. We only have to walk another mile to see evidence proving I'm most likely right. The closer we get to the river, the more everything looks like the old Ridderlands before the riders switched sides and created a paradise. There's a chance we get back only to find an empty river bed already destroyed by lava and boulders.

"We need to stop for a minute," I call out. Sue B and Barnaby have drifted ahead.

I kneel down and place a hand in the bristly dirt. When I don't feel any magic coursing through it, I try to push some of my magic down into the soil. The ground softens, and the prick of newly sprouting grass tickles my palm. When I move my hand, the grass continues to grow, and the area around it even brightens up as well.

"That's a relief," I say, more to myself than anyone else, but Sue B is close enough to hear.

"What is?"

"Whatever the reason things are dying here, my magic can be transferred back into the soil to help things flourish again."

"Do you have enough magic for all this acreage?" Barnaby asks.

"Even if I do, I don't have time to revive it all. I'll just have to hope it keeps on spreading," I answer.

We watch for a while longer until we're certain the effects are lasting, but we can't stay long. In fact, we only dare to stop to rest or drink water for a few minutes here and there along the way and to occasionally regenerate some green life. There are hours of walking ahead of us.

That is, until Sue B steps on a jagged bit of dried-out earth and twists her ankle. One minute she's leading the march back to the river, and the next she's rolling around on the ground in agony. I quickly magic everything I can think of to help her: ice packs, ace bandages, pain killers, crutches, and an ankle brace.

Barnaby pulls her sneaker and sock off to check for bruising and swelling. "Did you feel a pop? What about pain when I try to move it?"

Sue B shrieks as he turns her foot to the side.

"Help me get her up, Jessie. I need to see if she can bear any weight on it," he advises.

I do as he says, but it's not easy. I'm not tall enough or strong enough to give her much support. Luckily for all of us, Barnaby doesn't actually need my help at all. He hoists her up by her armpits while she leans on my shoulder with her left foot lifted.

"Try to take a step," Barnaby suggests.

Sue B glares at him but eventually sets her foot down like you would to dip your toes into a very hot bath to check the temp before getting in. She winces and pulls her leg away again.

"Did it hurt, or are you scared?" I ask. My sister isn't great with pain.

"Let me try again," she responds. This time she sets the foot flat to the ground, but she presses so firmly onto my shoulder for support, I almost crumple under her weight. "I…I can't do it," she says before yanking her foot up and away again.

Barnaby lowers her back down to the ground. "Let's try icing it for a bit and see how bad the swelling gets before we make any decisions."

"Wait a minute!" Sue B practically leaps up. "I know I'm usually the voice of reason—"

"Or the voice of doubt," I add, earning me a glare.

She continues. "But can't you heal my ankle like you've been healing the ground as we go?"

Whoa. Why didn't I think of that? Who needs modern medicine when you've got magical powers?

I crouch down next to her and wrap my hands gently around her swollen lump of an ankle. It must be super tender to the touch because her eyes are tearing up, and I'm barely applying any pressure. Rather than imagine her ankle healing, I do what I've been doing with the plants and push a little magic directly into the joint.

At first, when I move my hands, it looks like a big fail, but slowly the ankle shrinks, and the purple and red blotches fade back to her natural skin color.

"Try moving it around," Barnaby says.

She does one better and jumps up into a lunge. "It feels better than ever!"

Before I can think to celebrate, Sue B has wrapped me up in a huge embrace, then lifts me and spins me around like I'm four again.

"Okay, okay," I say. "You're welcome."

With the extra confidence from knowing that I can heal us if something goes wrong, we push forward toward the river, and a war bigger than any of us is ready for.

Chapter Thirty-One

The magic I pushed into the ground isn't moving quickly enough. We could wait for it to spread farther, making sure it reaches the river before we return, but the longer we wait, the more likely it is that Ritter will push across the minute he realizes the force field is no longer there. All it would take is one boulder to fly past the drying waterway without exploding against a shield for the war to be over before we get there.

We need to go faster.

"Slow down, Jessie!" Sue B yells after me.

I slow just enough to explain. "There's no time. We need to get back before Ritter realizes the magic has faded. It could already be too late."

She doesn't say anything else. Instead, she picks up her own pace, following my lead. The heavy pounding of Barnaby's boots tells me he's right behind her.

A too-familiar panic is rushing through me. Will I ever learn to stop racing toward problems, knowing I'll probably fail? No river means my ability to manipulate water is useless. No force field means no protection from the lava or the golems. And yet...

I don't think I'll ever shake the feeling that it's my job to save the world.

"Is that the river?" Barnaby shouts. "It's so..."

"Brown," Sue B finishes.

It takes me a few more steps before I see what they're seeing. "We're too late." I stop and fall to my knees—not even feeling the pain of the old wound I never bothered to heal; I really never think of myself.

"We can still fix this, Jess. There isn't any lava flowing across, and nothing's on fire. It's almost like he waited for us."

Sue B is right. Not about Ritter—or maybe she is—about fixing this. But I'll have to give it my all. Not only do I touch the ground, but I plant my fingers deep into the soil. If there was time to dig a hole, I would. This connection needs to be clear. The water is ready when I call out. It remembers the power I gave it at the dam, enough to carve up the ground, smooth a stone, or light up the world with electricity. Like snakes, I feel the streams and creeks slithering their way to the riverbed. Even the groundwater surges to the surface, ready to do its part.

"You're doing it," Barnaby cheers. "The river is refilling!"

But I don't stop there. I raise one hand to the sky and reach for the clouds while images of floods and mudslides fill my thoughts. We need rain, and lots of it. Enough to quench the fires and make the river overflow.

The first trickles land on my face and I look up to catch some in my mouth. Something I've done since I was little. What I see makes my heart skip a beat. "Look!" I gesture for Sue B and Barnaby to follow my gaze. High above us, dozens of ridders cut through the rain, heading for the battlegrounds.

"They must have sensed what you're doing." Barnaby's face is lit up like a little kid at Christmas.

"Thank goodness, I thought we were really going to have to fight this war," Sue B says, relieved.

"We still have to fight. We're not going to stand by and watch the ridders go at it alone. *I'm* not going to abandon them when I know my magic can help."

"Jessie, they abandoned us first. They brought us here and left us on the bank of the river with no way out and no warning that Ritter was alive and starting a war!" Her raised voice takes me by surprise.

I don't think I can hide the truth from her anymore. Not if I want her and Barnaby to trust the ridders and help them win control over this world for good. They don't deserve the anger she's aiming at them. She should be pointing that anger at me instead.

"It's my fault!"

"What are you talking about?" Sue B asks, rage still clinging to her words.

"I begged the ridders to bring us here. It's my fault we're trapped here and fighting for our lives."

"But you didn't have any magic. How is that even possible?" All the shine of hope in Barnaby's face is gone.

"I had a seed, saved all these years in my drawer. There was just enough magic in it to call out to them. But they didn't want to bring us. They only came because I said it was an emergency." There are tears trickling down my cheeks and mixing with the raindrops.

"Emergency? What the hell are you talking about, Jessie?" My sister is as mad as the day she banished me to this place.

"You—We weren't—Everything that happened with you and Barnaby, and you were mad at me because I took his side even though I didn't. I needed things to be better again because you're going away, and what if you were mad at me the whole time until you left? I'm terrified of losing you!"

Sue B grips her face in her hands but says nothing, and Barnaby approaches her but stops short, maybe unsure of how she'll react in this moment.

"I know you probably hate me now more than ever, but I'm telling you all this because we need to help the ridders. You can punish me when we're safe at home. Right now, we have a war to win."

Chapter Thirty-Two

I sprint away from them, faster than I've ever run. They'll eventually catch up, but it'll be too chaotic for them to force me to sit through some super intense lecture—or scream at me, then never speak to me ever again.

There are ridders perched on the ground and ridders flying overhead in circles. All of them are silent, waiting. Across the newly filled river is still mostly a blur of orange tones. I can't help but wonder why Ritter hasn't attacked yet.

Go no farther. The ridder's voice in my head takes me by surprise.

I nearly fall over, bringing myself to a stop. *Why is everyone waiting?* I ask back.

He waits for you.

For me? I'm the least important one here. The one who was sent here once by accident and twice more only because I forced my way. Sue B and Barnaby are the two he's always been after. Sure, I've got the magic—can create things in this world—but that's only because I'm the youngest, right? I'm not special. I'm just Susan Beezly's little sister. Always trailing behind her.

Except now. I look back and remember I'm the one in the lead. Even though the choices I made to get us here are wrong, helping to free this world—and the ridders—is the right thing to do.

"What's happening?" Sue B asks through panting breaths.

"The ridders told me to stop."

"Good. At least someone can talk some sense into you," she adds.

"They say that Ritter is waiting for me."

"And that's exactly why you need to stay away. I'm not letting you get yourself killed, even if it's your own fault that we're here."

"Go easy on her, Sue B." I'm shocked that Barnaby isn't furious with me.

"Why should I? Of all the dumb things she's done, this takes the cake."

"Because we've *all* made huge mistakes that brought us here. We've all risked our lives following one another on some absurd adventure in this world. She's younger than you were when you started all this. Sure, it's easy to look back now and realize how crazy we were—dumb—but hindsight is twenty-twenty."

"Fine," Sue B concedes. "But I'm still not letting her rush into battle! She's my baby sister!"

"Could anything have stopped us back then?" he asks. "We were always so sure we were doing the right thing."

She looks into the distance, surveying the river and the waiting army. Then she grabs both of our hands. "If we're going to fight, we're doing it how we've always done it. Together."

We move forward like the characters in *The Wizard of Oz* going down the yellow brick road—minus the skipping. Perhaps the weirdest possible way to approach an army. The ridders don't try to stop us this time. Instead, the ones on the ground take flight to follow. I'd say they're our flying monkeys, except the monkeys worked for the witch, I think. Anyway, forget the movie. This is scarier and more real than any movie could be.

The ridders start screeching the nearer we get, which makes my heart pound so much I feel like a bomb. And just as I think I might explode, the biggest boulder I've ever seen shatters into a million pieces and we all dive for the ground. Thank goodness the force field is still in place.

"Everyone okay?" Barnaby asks as he gets back to his feet.

Sue B and I nod, though I grip my aching knee. It's time to heal this stupid thing. But before I can focus on the magic, another explosion blasts overhead. There's no time.

"How close to the river do you need to be?" Sue B asks. "Can you control the water from here?"

I try reaching for the water like I did at the dam and like I did to fill the river, but I can't make a connection. "It's not working. I don't understand. Let's get closer."

When I lift my hands from the ground, they're shaking. It takes my sister's touch to stop the trembling. Before we move on, I grip my aching knee to relieve my pain. It's stupid I haven't taken a minute to heal myself, knowing how hard the fight ahead of us will be.

"Give me a second," I tell Sue B. A sharp pain shoots through my leg, making sure I don't forget about it again. My eyes close, and I channel magic into my fingertips, pushing what I can into the bruised tissue and swelling. There's a light tingling sensation that tickles the skin before buzzing deeper into the surface. It reminds me of the numbing shot from the dentist before he did my filling last year. I don't have time to wait until the swelling goes down to make sure it worked, so I push myself up and take off again ahead of Sue B and Barnaby.

Chapter Thirty-Three

"Stop…running…ahead," Sue B yells after me, her words broken between breaths, half annoyance and half concern.

Overhead, a loud screech catches my attention. One of the ridders dives from his position over the river as a fireball rises high above us like an asteroid from space. By instinct, I duck to the ground with my arms protecting my head. Dumb for two reasons: 1. Dinosaurs might still be here if duck and cover worked against giant space rocks of fire. 2. It's already been confirmed that the force field still works.

I laugh at myself as I get back to my feet and turn to see both Sue B and Barnaby cowering in the grass. Instincts are hard to fight.

"It's kind of like fireworks when they shatter at the force field," I say to them.

They peek their heads up and see the bits of rock, glowing like ashes and embers, raining down. We're far enough away for now not to get burned or pelted by the fragments that are small enough to get through, but we have to get closer for my magic to be any help, which puts us at risk of injuries.

What we need is something to protect us, like Barnaby's hoodie when we first arrived, or like the canopies of the trees did later on. Similar to an umbrella but stronger. Light enough to carry but durable.

Shields!

I hold out my forearm, like a Spartan from the movies, and I imagine the perfect shield building around my arm. Bits of leather and metal and wood forming a circular guard to fit me precisely. When I trust that it's complete, I open my eyes and hold it over me, blocking out the sky easily.

Then I ask Barnaby to do the same. I want each of their shields to feel custom-made for them. Just like mine.

"Imagine the shield you want," I tell him.

"This is incredible," Barnaby shouts. His shield looks like it's pulled from a King Arthur legend—shiny and polished. "Better than any online RPG."

"RP what?" Sue B asks.

"Duh! He's talking about role-playing games. The kind of thing you suck at."

"I've already had enough adventure for a lifetime. Why would I spend my time in the real world creating make-believe danger?"

"Because it's fun," Barnaby and I answer in unison.

"Shield me," she says, ignoring us. Her arm is held in front of her like she's churning butter at the pioneer village or something.

With the three shields finished, it's clear which of us were focused on our visions and which weren't. Sue B's is a simple, square board of wood. There are twigs sticking out in places and knots where the wood was damaged.

She's got her head tilted on its side as she takes it in. "Did I do something wrong?"

"Magic is all about believing and committing your imagination. Either you still don't trust it, or you're the least creative person in the world," I tease.

Barnaby grips her shoulder. "As long as it keeps you safe. I don't think anyone is scoring on aesthetics." It seems like he's trying to comfort her, except that he covers his mouth as he walks away, shoulders shaking.

The murmurs of the ridders are growing louder around us, so I tune in to see if I can pick up anything being said. There are too many conversations going on at once. Only bits and pieces of words are coming through. *Fire...stolen...boom...barrier...destroy...*

Are they going to destroy the golems, or are the golems going to destroy the barrier? And what's stolen? The fire?

Sue B stays close by my side as we approach a group of trees no more than fifty feet away from the river's shore. "Try your magic again," she suggests.

This time, when I reach for the ground, picturing the water's power, I feel the familiar tug of connection. Almost like the water is begging for my help to rise up against Ritter. It wants to fight. "I can feel it. We're close enough," I tell my sister.

"What about the rock golems? Can you feel their magic too?" Barnaby asks.

I try, but when I hit the force field, the barrier keeps me from probing beyond the invisible wall. "I can't sense anything beyond the river. How are we supposed to break their connection with Ritter if I can't touch the magic that brought them to life?"

"We're going to have to find another way. There's a chance I could take Ritter out physically," says Barnaby. "I bet I'm much bigger than him now."

"That might be true if he was a regular person, but with his magic, you'd be putting yourself in serious danger." Sue B crosses her arms and tightens her lips. She's definitely not on board with Barnaby's macho suggestion.

It doesn't matter if it's a good idea because a major quake shifts the ground beneath us and sends us all tipping over like bowling pins. And this time, the shaking doesn't stop after a minute, making me lose all sense of time while the tremors continue. We each crawl away from the trees, afraid of what will happen if a branch breaks or the tree is uprooted.

But something much, much worse happens than a damaged tree. When the quaking stops, and we can finally stand up again, the river is where the real problem lies.

"What happened?" I yell, not believing what I'm seeing.

"Remember the earthquake that opened up the chasm that we escaped through the first time we left this place?" Barnaby and I nod at Sue B. "Well, sometimes earthquakes cause the ground to separate like that, but sometimes two chunks of land crash against each other and one is pushed up to relieve the pressure."

"The water's stopped flowing where the river bed's risen. Something's happening with the magic." I can feel the change.

Chapter Thirty-Four

"The force field—it's failing!"

"What do you mean *failing*?" Barnaby asks.

"Without the water, the boundary is disappearing. It's not protected anymore."

The ridders are practically screaming as they realize the same horrible thing. *Water...the water...the water is going!*

"But you can control the water," Sue B says. "Can't you fix it?"

"And make the water flow up the ridge? Isn't that like gravitatily impossible?"

"First of all, that's not a word. And second, are we talking about physics or are we talking about magic?" She has a point.

Before I can try, a golden eruption bubbles up at the river's edge, lava wasting no time trying to fill the space as the water falls away from the risen area.

"Are we too late?" Sue B wonders.

"I have to try."

More lava is spewing from the crack in the ground. Blobs of it splattering then sizzling against the water that's pooling away. It glows against the dark purple sky.

"Hurry! It'll be across the river in no time." My sister sounds so afraid.

There's a loud CRACK! followed by a bright flash from the mountainside where more magma is waiting to release. I have to act fast.

Kneeling to touch the ground, I reconnect with the now-wounded water and remind it of its power, trying to rebuild its confidence. "Push back!" I whisper. I try to imagine waterfalls rushing upward instead of falling down, and I feel the water building—slowly like a boiling pot. "More. Push harder."

Water splashes up against the rock face of the shifted land, ignoring gravity, each droplet a salmon going upstream. But it's not enough. Every rush of water comes tumbling back down.

"It's not working," I shout in frustration.

"So use that creativity of yours. You're the same girl who made a plastic slide carve down a cliff so you could get back to me with Barnaby."

It's so much harder to do this under pressure. How can I get the water to do something so inconceivable? Why couldn't the other side of the river have been the one to push upward? Maybe it's just not possible. The ridders won't land since the lava erupted. In fact, they're flying higher, probably worried about the fireballs that luckily have stopped for now. If they can't do anything to fix this, what makes me think I can?

"I can't—"

"You can," Barnaby insists. "We just need an idea."

"What if you reverse the flow? There has to be a waterway at the mouth of the river. Maybe that can act as a source. If it comes from the other direction, you don't need to fight gravity."

"Is that normally possible?" I ask my sister. "You're the science guru."

"I think I read somewhere that the Mississippi River once flowed in reverse." She shrugs.

I look to the water to see how much worse things have gotten while we brainstormed. There's a thin stream of the stuff burning across the grass on our side of the bank. It's now or never. The water hasn't stopped trying to climb the wall when I reach back with my magic and ask it to find its ending and call it here. The mouth of the river is too far away for me to connect, but I have to hope the water shares a bond I'll never understand. Two parts of a whole that are longing to be one again.

At first, it's a trickle, too weak to survive the lava pouring across. But soon enough, the river's desire to reunite is stronger than the intense heat of the magma. I've done it. Wherever the mouth of the river is, the water must be cold. Hissing sounds fill the air like a million angry cats surrounding us. A dense fog from the hot steam fills the air. It's so thick we can't see across to the other side.

We don't see Ritter use the distraction to his advantage.

Chapter Thirty-Five

With the water restored, the ridders fly in, forming a weaving pattern in the air. Their acrobatics are amazing to watch while they try to restore the force field. I can feel its power building with every swoop of flight.

Then suddenly there is a burst of fire. We watch in stunned disbelief as a ridder is knocked from the sky by a flaming boulder bigger than anything they should be able to launch. I'm rushing to the injured ridder's side when another crashes to the ground mere feet away from where I'm standing. Explosion after explosion, more ridders are hurtled to the ground, forcing the rest to retreat. But without the full force field working, there's nothing to protect any of us from the rock golems' destruction. With the steam, we can't even tell where they're aiming.

I'm thinking we're doomed as I take in the surrounding battlefield. Some of the ridders are able to shake off their injuries, but others aren't moving at all, and I fear the worst. The reality that we could die here hits harder than ever. But there might be one good thing about the magical shield being down.

"I need you two to shield me and let me know if we need to make a run for it."

"Why?" Sue B asks.

"There's no time to explain. Can you do it?" They nod their assent.

I take in a few deep breaths to center myself and remove the outside distraction of blasts and panicked screeches. It's hard to ignore what's going on around me, but I need to be focused if this is going to work. With all the concentration I can muster, I plant my fingers into the soil below me and reach for the magic that controls the rock golems. Visions of settled mountains and peaceful rock formations fill my mind. Not because I'm willing the golems to go back to sleep, but because they are longing to rest. Like the ridders before them, it seems the golems are being forced to fight us. Every boulder that launches or shatters increases their exhaustion and their mourning.

If I could get them to listen, would they lay down their weapons? Trying is the only way I'll know. *You don't have to fight.* My words meet resistance. Something—or someone—is blocking them out.

"Barnaby, do you still feel ready to distract Ritter?"

He lowers his shield and looks to Sue B, who is frantically shaking her head no.

"If we're going to have any hope of winning this war, I need to draw Ritter's attention away from the golems. I think I have a way to end this."

"There's still enough fog for me to sneak across the river, but how am I supposed to find him?" Barnaby asks.

A voice in my head interrupts us. *I will take him. I can find him.* It's the injured ridder to my left, and I run over to speak with her.

"But you're hurt."

Only my wing. I can walk. I can jump.

"Are you sure?"

We do it together.

"What's going on? What are they saying?" Barnaby wonders.

"She's going to carry you across and bring you to Ritter."

The two of them creep away in a crouch to the far right side of the river. I'm scared for my friends, but I trust them.

"What do we do?" My sister goes back to biting her nails.

"I need you to keep me safe while I work my magic." I wink at her and hope the humor in my statement distracts her from her worry. "I've gotta get closer so my connection to the rock golems is as strong as possible, and your shield will blend right into our surroundings."

We are across, the ridder informs me.

"They made it to the other side. Are you ready to move?" Sue B nods like she doesn't have a choice. And we don't. We've got to do this.

Chapter Thirty-Six

Despite most of the ridders fleeing high into the sky where they are out of reach from the fireballs, the rock golems keep launching their attack. Trees burn everywhere around us. If the golems could see Sue B and me, I'm sure we'd be dead by now. The chaos and low visibility are our only advantages.

My sister suggests we army crawl, but it would take too long to get out of the way if a lucky shot found us. In fact, there's almost no reason we can't just make a run for it. My only concern is Ritter sensing me coming because of my magic. But surely even he's too distracted with everything going on to focus on me. So we run. And, hopefully for the last time. Though my knee is healed, I'm exhausted from the journey back to the river and lightheaded from breathing in the ash and smoke that gets worse with every fireball.

I can tell it's taking its toll on Sue B too. She's trying to be strong, maybe for me, but I've never seen her more scared in this place than she is right now. Her hands are trembling, nails bitten down to bleeding. Her eyes are bright and wet with the threat of tears. I need to end this for all of us.

At the river's edge, I probe for the magic that connects the golems to Ritter and find it easily. Barnaby must not have found Ritter yet because the connection is unwavering.

"Now what?" Sue B asks in a whisper.

"Now, we wait for Barnaby to draw Ritter's attention so I can convince the golems to resist."

This close to the river, I can hear the rock golems moving, their thunderous steps and the tearing of rock from the mountainside. There's a sound like a rockslide that goes on for several minutes, but we see no evidence of one happening. It's only when the fireballs stop flying overhead that I can guess at what might have occurred. I reach back into the magic to test my theory. Ritter has released his puppets. The rock golems have collapsed.

"It's time," I whisper to Sue B. I close my eyes, ignoring the panic I see rise in her face.

The rocky giants aren't simple boulders yet; they've only been set to rest like a child discarding his toys to stop for lunch. I push my magic into them, waking them just enough to hear my words.

You must resist if you want to settle back to stone. Walk away now. Harden and be at peace. I will protect you.

We will protect you. In unison, several ridders add their voices to my offer.

He not let rest, the rock golems respond. *Never let go.*

Now is your chance. You can be free of his power, but you have to go now. We will stop him. Please! I flood our connection with pictures of mountains, beautiful and still, hoping they'll take a chance.

One of the golems pulls at my magic as he rises. It takes so much effort to move just one of these creatures. Then a burst of power supports my energy. The ridders are joining me. We can only do this together.

"It's working," I say to Sue B through gritted teeth.

We go. Meant to sleep. With the leader's words, the rest of the golems use our combined magic to march away.

The shaking of their retreat is sure to catch Ritter's attention, but we can't let him interfere. All of our hope rests with Barnaby and the ridder who went with him. I have to check in.

Have you taken out Ritter?

There's no answer.

Friends, can you sense your sister? Maybe the other ridders can reach her.

The answer is a knife to the chest. *Sister is gone.*

Barnaby!

Without thinking, I dive into the river and swim as quickly as I can across, leaving my own sister stuck behind me. I climb onto the shore and feel through the dense fog around me for some kind of landmark. A cliff's edge or boulder to orient myself around.

"Ritter!" I scream into the sky. "Ritter!"

The fog parts in front of me like Moses and the sea. There's a grin on his face despite losing all his weapons. A sinking feeling hits my stomach, and I suddenly have the urge to puke. Is this a trap? Is this what he wanted?

Face-to-face with my nemesis, I roll my shoulders back and swallow my fear. I'm not going down without a fight. And unlike him, I'm not alone. We will end this and make sure he never harms this world—or mine—ever again.

"What did you do to Barnaby?" My words are venom.

"Did you really think he could overpower me? That I would succumb to brute strength alone?"

"Give him back and maybe I'll go easy on you."

His laugh makes my blood boil. He doesn't think I'll be a challenge.

I imagine myself as a snake, coiling up in warning, hissing and swaying before I lunge. When the picture is so clear and so real that I can nearly feel the fangs in my mouth, I burst toward him with all my magic's intent. I feel my venom flow through as the teeth of my magic sink into his flesh. Around me, I can sense the bite of ridders latching onto him with their own power.

Ritter sinks to his knees as we drain him.

"I have one thing that you'll never have," I say, withdrawing to let the ridders finish the job. "I have allies who fight with me as a team, not because they're forced to, but because they're willing. I have love and friendship and family. I have the power of what's right on my side. As long as we have people who care enough to stand with us, we will always be stronger than you."

As Ritter writhes on the ground he begins to shrink, further and further until he is nothing more than a speck of dust in the dry wasteland he created.

Chapter Thirty-Seven

Now that he's gone, I need to find Barnaby and get back to Sue B before she drowns herself trying to cross the river to find us.

"Barnaby!" I call as loudly as I can. Much easier now that the explosions and eruptions have ended. "Barnaby!" When there's no answer, I know I need help searching. *Do you know where my friend is? I'm sorry you've lost yours.*

We will take you. And the other.

Several ridders rise a few feet into the air and waft their wings to clear the smoke and fog. The wind they create is intense, reminding me of the whirlwind they used to try to rip us from the ground the first time we came to the Ridderlands. A ridder approaches me, using his wings to block me from blowing away. Once the air is clear enough for them to stop, he asks me to climb onto his back and takes flight across the river. I see Sue B below us waving her arms in the air as if we'll miss her.

"Thank God you're okay," she says in relief when we land.

"Now let's make sure Barnaby is," I respond. "Climb on."

The ridder takes off again, but this time he flies higher and higher, and I'm not sure where he's taking us, only that wherever it is, Barnaby will be there. My insides twist and turn with the thought of what we might find. I don't want to admit the possibility that he's—

"What happened with Ritter?" my sister asks.

"We don't ever have to worry about him again." I don't add details, and she doesn't ask for them. Right now, all that matters is finding Barnaby and getting home.

We land on the edge of a cliff that's high above the battlefield below. The perfect vantage point to carry out his attacks—I can tell immediately why Ritter picked it.

"Barnaby, are you here?" Neither of us waits for him to answer me. There's a cave at the back of the cliff that is disturbingly quiet. I look over my shoulder at Sue B and we enter the dark space without hesitation.

"Barnaby?" Sue B's voice is low and shaky.

"I'm going farther in. He has to be here."

Twenty steps into the pitch black nothingness and I go flying forward, tripping over something on the floor of the cave. As I feel around on the cold stone for whatever made me lose my footing, I come across the soft fabric of Barnaby's hoodie and his limp arm within it.

"Sue B, he's here." Only then do I remember my magic and create an orb of light to brighten the cave so she can find us.

"He's unconscious," she murmurs.

"But he's breathing, so he's alive." I hover my hands over his chest and press the orb of light into him. I'm not sure what makes me do it, just another instinct I follow without thinking.

Barnaby's chest lifts into the air, and his body begins to glow. When he opens his eyes, two beams of light shoot out like lasers before all the light disappears, and he settles back to the ground.

"What happened?" we hear in the dark. Barnaby is awake. Barnaby is alive and okay.

The next thing I feel is Sue B's arms wrapping us both up.

Walking hand in hand, we exit the cave together and rejoin the ridder who flew us here.

"What do we do now?" Sue B asks.

"We go home."

We will take you now, the ridder tells me. *But you can never return.*

"What's he saying?" Barnaby asks.

"They're going to bring us home but—"

We are closing the opening to your world. There cannot be another like him.

Like who?

"Jessie?" I ignore Barnaby.

Ritter.

I don't understand. He came from our world? But his magic?

He was a child, lost and alone. His magic was a gift from us. We cared for him, and he grew to betray us. Betrayed his own people.

"OMG!"

"What is it, Jessie?"

I finally answer them. Explaining everything the ridder just told me.

"I can't believe it," Sue B says. "How could someone be so awful?"

"He was just a kid, and no one came looking for him. He had no reason to care for his home world." Barnaby is so good at empathizing. Even with this monster.

"But the ridders cared for him, gave him magic, and he used it against them too!" Sue B argues.

"Maybe whatever happened to him before he came here scarred him. Made him think everyone would abandon him—hurt him. There's no way for us to ever know. I'm not saying that justifies what he did— everything he's done was horrible and his own choice—but if this place has taught us anything, it's that things aren't always what they appear."

"You're right, Barnaby."

"I think it's time we put this world behind us," Sue B says.

"Time to go home," I add.

Chapter Thirty-Eight

Just like every other time we've returned, we end up in bed with a new day welcoming us home. But never before have I felt so lucky to be given another day. And I know exactly what I want to focus on from now on.

Finding me.

I look around my room. Taking in all the ways that Sue B has shaped my personality all these years through the treasures we've shared: posters, knickknacks, music, books. Maybe it's time for a change—time for a clean slate.

The posters come down first. Every single one is a favorite movie or band that my sister introduced me to. I even take down the ones that I'd probably have liked without her, given the freedom to explore my own tastes. I can always come back to them.

But posters are easy compared to the hand-me-down stuffed animals I've slept with for years or the collection of nail polish we've built together.

There's a knock at my door that interrupts my thoughts. I toss the matted unicorn stuffy I've been holding back onto the bed and answer, expecting Dad ready with jokes and announcing breakfast. Instead, Sue B is standing there in some oversized sweatpants, a ratty tee, and a messy bun tangled on the top of her head.

"What are you doing in here?" she asks. "I heard you banging around from down the hall."

"Sorry if I woke you up. I'll try to keep the noise down."

"It's fine," Sue B says, then she invites herself in and crashes onto my bed.

"Wait, aren't you mad at me?" I ask.

She doesn't sit up, just flaps her hands at me like it's all no big deal.

"I could have gotten you killed, Sue B—you and Barnaby."

"Maybe you're forgetting that I once banished you to the Ridderlands because I thought you were annoying. Barnaby was right. You didn't do anything worse than what we did, and you were trying to help."

"So you forgive me?"

"Of course, I forgive you. You're my little sister." She picks up the unicorn I was just messing with. "I can't believe you still have this," she says, holding him up. "I gave him to you when we got back from that world the first time. My own version of an apology."

"Actually, I was considering getting rid of him—rid of everything."

"So that's what's going on. Erasing all evidence of me as your sister or…?"

"It's not like that."

"I know." She laughs. "I'm only teasing. I get what you're doing. I think it's a good thing. I can't wait to come back during my first break and see the new you. And if you're getting rid of this guy, maybe he could come with me—help me remember you."

"Is it okay if I'm still not ready to talk about you leaving?" I ask.

"Yeah. I get it."

There's a heavy silence that takes a while to settle enough for a subject change. Sue B plays with the unicorn, and I listen to Mom and Dad starting their day downstairs.

"So what are you going to do about prom?"

"Do we have to talk about that?" Sue B curls her lip and wrinkles her nose.

"We don't have to. It's your business, but you should know that Barnaby basically admitted to me that he's totally in love with you."

She pulls the unicorn over her face to hide and kicks her legs. "Why can't he just tell me that?"

"He's kind of a coward, sis. Like a meek little mouse."

Sue B sits up. "Ugh…you're right. Why are you always right?"

"*Almost* always," I say. "I did make a horrible mistake recently."

"Touché. We're all allowed a lapse in judgment from time to time."

"Well…"

"Fiiiinneeeee. I'll call him."

I climb up on the bed next to her, and she hands me an earbud. Not to interfere, but to hear what happens. I've learned my lesson.

Chapter Thirty-Nine

"Hello."

"Hey."

"Hey. You both okay?"

"We're good," Sue B says. I giggle in the background. Sue B hushes me with a finger to her lips.

"I heard—"

"I wanted to—"

Of course, they both start talking at the same time.

"You go," Sue B says.

"Okay, well. I wanted to apologize because I know you overheard Ana talking about me asking Hillary to the dance."

A tear pools in the corner of my sister's eye. I didn't realize it would be this hard for her to face her problem after everything we all went through together. I thought it would be easier.

"Yeah," is all she can get out.

"The whole thing—it was…a mistake. I wasn't going to go to prom with anyone."

"Oh."

"Not because I didn't want to!"

He's really messing this whole thing up.

"I wanted to go with you. I've always imagined going with you. Sue B, you have to know how much I…grrr. This is so hard to say to you.

Okay. I'm just going to say it. I've liked you for a really, really long time, Sue B. Like, so much. I was never planning on asking Hillary to the dance. This is all Nick's fault—and Ana's—and mine for not explaining earlier."

"Can you please just tell me what's going on?" Sue B says impatiently. Maybe just hurt. I can't tell the difference.

"Nick asked me to help *him* ask Hillary to the prom. I ended up planning the whole thing because Nick is a complete idiot. I asked Ana to help me make the sign, and she got the wrong idea, assuming it was for me. I don't know why I didn't realize the mistake sooner, or why I didn't just explain it to you before it became this huge issue."

"You expect me to believe that it's just a misunderstanding?"

"Well, yeah. Because it's true."

"You know he's a terrible liar," I whisper.

"And the sign you made for me? Is that the same one you made for Hillary too?"

"Crap."

"Are you serious?!" Sue B yells.

"Well, like I said, I wasn't going to go to prom with anyone. I was too scared that if I asked you and you didn't feel the same way, you'd hate me and never speak to me again. I couldn't bear the thought of losing you completely in my life. It would be too easy with us both leaving for college for you to cut me out. But when I was making the poster for Nick, I started thinking about you and what if you said yes—what if you did feel the same way."

"So you recycled the poster Nick used for Hillary?"

"Not exactly. More like I stole the sign I made for him. I told Nick to figure out his own promposal, and I used the one I planned to ask you. You were the inspiration for it all along."

Now Sue B is legitimately crying. "Do you mean it?"

"I'm obviously in love with you, Susan Beezly!" I can't believe Barnaby just blurts it out.

My sister's cheeks flare as red as Taylor Swift's lips. I feel super uncomfortable listening in to the rest of their conversation, so I pop out the earbud and sneak out of the room.

Chapter Forty

The end of August

Sue B stands in my bedroom doorway, her suitcases on the ground by her side. I rise from my bed, where I've been crying quietly to myself since last night, and hand her the unicorn stuffed animal. One of only a few things I decided to keep after clearing out my room.

"You sure you don't want to keep him?" she asks.

"I'm more worried about you forgetting me than me forgetting you," I say.

She leans forward and cups my cheek with one hand while wiping away a tear with the other. "I could never, ever forget you, Jessie. You're basically my favorite person in this world—any world." She winks.

It gets a chuckle out of me. I snort in to clear my nose. "Even more than Barnaby?" I tease. The two of them have been practically inseparable since we got back. Which means I've had to split all the time I've had left with Sue B with both Barnaby and Hillary.

"More than Barnaby."

"I'm really gonna miss you," I blurt. Then I bury my face in her chest.

"Not as much as I'll miss you. Which is why I convinced Mom and Dad to give you this." Sue B hands me a brand new phone.

"Are you serious?! A phone?"

"I told them it was absolutely necessary that I be able to call you directly, anytime I needed you. And maybe, even though you've been busy exploring all the ways we're different and developing some truly terrible tastes in movies, you might need to call your big sister from time to time too."

"Sueba Sueba Doo, we're gonna be late if we don't get out the door now. You've got a plane to catch." I shoot eye daggers at Dad from upstairs for interrupting us.

"Are you sure you don't want to come to drop me off at the airport?" she asks.

"And risk seeing someone I know while I'm bawling my eyes out on the sidewalk? It's better we say goodbye here," I say, swiping my hand across my eyes.

"Call me anytime, promise?" Sue B says. Then she wipes her own reddening eyes.

I nod intently.

We embrace one more time, holding onto each other until Mom and Dad start threatening to leave without her.

"I love you, Jessie Jess."

"I love you too, Sue B, forever."

Acknowledgments

Wow, the series is at an end, and I'm really going to miss these characters. No one tells you when you start writing a series that they will end up meaning as much to you as some of the real relationships you have. From Sue B I've learned forgiveness and commitment, from Barnaby I've learned to love myself even on my worst days and to take time to heal, and from Jessie Jess, the heroine of this last story, I'm reminded of the feisty girl I used to be—struggling to find her place in this world—and I give myself permission to be unapologetically fierce when I need to be.

Thanks to my family for sticking with me through the brainstorms, the meltdowns, and the times I thought I'd never finish. Your love and care mean everything to me. We did it!

Thank you to my editor, Shawn Simmons, for your patience as we finish this series together. To Rachel Fitzjames for the constant support as I struggled to make room for creativity during a year of hardship, your encouragement kept me pushing forward, even if it was a few words at a time. To the writer friends I've made along the way on this crazy publishing journey, you exist all over the world, but your passion and love is felt every day—with a special nod to Jaime Formato, Gretchen Filart, and Emma Perry. And lastly, thank you for all of the expertise at Level Best Books that went into making *The Ridders* series a reality.

About the Author

Melissa Ruth Rotert is a poet turned writer of speculative fiction for all ages. She lives in Western NY and is an avid Buffalo Bills fan who enjoys exploring every day with her family and editing short fiction with *Epistemic Literary Magazine* and *Nimblewitlit*. When she's not writing or reading, she's snuggled up with her two rescue dogs and any number of foster pups.

AUTHOR WEBSITE:

  melruthwrites.com

BLOG:

  https://onpunsandneedles.godaddysites.com/

SOCIAL MEDIA HANDLES:
@MelRuthWrites- Bluesky
@melruthwrites- IG

Also by Melissa Ruth Rotert

The Ridder Series books 1 & 2:
Sue B and The Ridders
The Return of Ritter

Short Stories:
"These Houses Would Sing," *INKbabies Literary Magazine* Issue 1-Fall/Summer
"Lindy Bird Fly," *OxMag Literary Journal* July '22 Issue 48
"The Whiskey Voice," *Tenpenny Dreadfuls: Tales as Hard as Nails* anthology;
Several pieces with *Flash Fiction Magazine*